DISOWNED

ALSO BY
M.J. HAAG

FAIRY TALE RETELLINGS
(ALL IN THE SAME WORLD)

BEASTLY TALES

Depravity

Deceit

Devastation

TALES OF CINDER

Disowned (prequel)

Defiant

Disdain

Damnation

RESURRECTION CHRONICLES
(hottie demons!)

Demon Ember	*Demon Escape*	*Demon Dawn*
Demon Flames	*Demon Deception*	*Dmeon Disgrace*
Demon Ash	*Demon Night*	*Demon Fall*

DISOWNED

TALES OF CINDER AND SNOW

A PREQUEL

M.J. HAAG

Shattered Glass
—PUBLISHING—

ISBN 978-1-943051-10-6 (eBook Edition)
ISBN 978-1-943051-41-0 (Paperback Edition)

Editing by Ulva Eldridge
Cover design by Shattered Glass Publishing LLC

Version 2021.02.13

*To those before me who created the original tales
on which these retellings are based.
To the readers who loved them enough to want more.
To the magic found in our imaginations.*

CHAPTER ONE

"Margaret, hold still."

I struggled to do as Mother asked. The lace on my cuffs was making my arm itch.

She wound a thick strand of my dark hair up to the top of my head and pinned it in place. In the mirror, I stared at my reflection. Mother was almost done.

"Are there any biscuits left?" I asked.

"You'll be covered in crumbs."

"An apple then?"

"There will be food later."

"Food that I can hold but not eat for fear of a speck marring my perfection." My pleasant tone didn't soften the disapproval in my words.

Mother gave me a cross look as she pinned the last strand into place.

"You act as if we are cruel to you, when we only ask what all parents ask. Marriage will ensure you have a home and a family to call your own."

"This is not my home? You are not my family?"

She tsked.

"Go eat your apple, willful child. Remember my graciousness when you consider mischief tonight. And keep yourself clean."

"Yes, Mother." I gave her a quick curtsy and exited the room, keeping the mischievous smile from my lips. I wasn't hungry for an apple, only an excuse to escape.

Keeping my steps measured, I maintained the picture of poise and beauty as I made my way down the staircase. Father's study doors were closed. Stepping softly, I swiftly passed them and went to the kitchen.

"You look lovely, Miss Margaret," Judith said a bit too loudly. The cook ignored us both, her focus on the spices in the cabinet.

"Mother said I could have an apple. Are there any?"

"No apples. Only pears."

"That will have to do."

Judith smirked and, with an obedient bob of her head, went to the cold storage. She was the closest thing I had to a friend. She knew I wasn't like the rest. Whatever wealth or title my family possessed, it did not change how I viewed my position in life. It did not give me the right to look down upon or mistreat others.

However, I was not yet free to make my own rules and openly befriend Judith. Doing so would cause her dismissal. No matter how I thought of myself, it was how my parents thought of me that mattered. And they thought me above mingling with the servants.

She returned with the pear. I accepted it from her with a smile.

"Thank you, Judith."

She nodded and glanced at the cook. I waited until she smiled to bite into the pear and wandered toward the door.

I grabbed her cloak and eased it over my shoulders. I knew she wouldn't mind me borrowing it, and the cover would hopefully hide the majority of my cream skirt. As soon as I had it on, I called to the Cook.

"Please inform my parents that I will meet them at the House of Greylin."

I opened the door and slipped outside before the cook could react. Lifting my skirts, I ran. My passage startled several of the stable hands.

I raced through the yard and out onto the cobbled streets where horse-drawn carriages moved slowly through the light foot traffic. The nearest startled at my sudden appearance. I chuckled as the well-dressed man struggled for control.

It took several minutes before I reached the smaller homes further away from the castle. Ducking onto a dirt path between two houses, I pulled up my hood. A running servant wouldn't be noticed here, but a well-bred young woman might.

I continued walking at a brisk pace, competing with the darkening sky.

A curl of purple-grey smoke rising from the chimney of a thatched roof house heralded the end of my journey. I knocked on the wide-planked door and waited. It swung open only a moment later. The scents of herbs and the tingle of magic greeted me.

Elspeth grinned when I lifted my head to peer at her from under the hood of the cloak.

"Well, come in, imp. What trouble do you have in mind this time?"

"Trouble?" I asked innocently.

"If it's about the beauty spell again—"

I waved my hand as she closed the door behind me.

"As much as I would love the world to see the true Aleese, I understand why you cannot sell a bad spell. Your magic is your livelihood because you're the best at what you do. Which is why I'm here. I want you to make me ugly." I removed my cloak and hung it on a peg beside her door. "Not hideously. Just unattractive yet recognizable to someone not blinded by their own self-worth."

"Child, I question your purpose. I thought you despised those who changed their appearance."

"I don't mean to make myself homely permanently. Only for tonight."

Her face swept over me, lingering on my dress and coiffed hair.

"The house of Cresstoll?"

"No. Lord Greylin's this time. All the girls are ever so hopeful to win the attention of strapping Brendal."

"I thought his interest lay with Feshell and your mother was determined to see you with the Cresstoll boy."

"She was until she discovered I was stuffing my waistline and never lifting my head enough for him to see my face. Now, I believe she's determined to prance me in front of Brendal. She's given me strict orders not to stuff my waistline this time."

Elspeth shook her head at me.

"Being beautiful isn't a tragedy, Margaret."

"It is if it means you must marry a shallow sop."

"Your parents will know it was me. There will be repercussions."

"Please, Elspeth. Mother doesn't care if Brendal is a decent man, only that he will inherit the title of Lord. I just need to separate the chaff from the grain. This spell is the only way."

"And if there is only chaff?"

"That would suit me well."

"You know you need to choose soon. Your seventeenth year isn't far away."

I snorted and moved to the chair beside the fire, already knowing that I'd won.

"You're starting to sound like my mother," I commented.

Elspeth grinned.

"I have saved you from your own foolishness more times than I can count. While I find the antics that vex your parents amusing, sounding like your mother might not be amiss. You need to think of your future, Margaret."

She paused and gave me a hard look that hid the affection I knew she felt for me.

"I most definitely am thinking of my future."

"So be it. Payment is required."

"Of course."

I withdrew a blunt silver from my pocket.

"Is this enough?"

"Barely."

We both knew it was plenty for the simple spell. Just as we knew she would use the money to buy food to help those less fortunate on the outskirts of town.

She tucked away the coin and went to her herbs and potions.

"Temporary glamours I have in plenty. But all for enhanced beauty. Margaret, you are the first to ask to be made ugly."

"I wish you weren't opposed to making someone else ugly."

"As much as I would enjoy seeing a bit of retribution on a few of those twits, it is not worth the risk. Never forget—"

"All magic done with malicious intent on another has a high cost," I said with her. "I know. It doesn't stop me from wishing, though."

I remained quiet as she mixed a potion and spoke quietly while holding it over a bowl of clear water to prove our intent and the potion pure.

When she finished, she handed me the vial.

"It will last three hours from when you drink it."

I tipped it back, and she groaned.

"It will not last the whole evening now."

A tingle ran through me, tickling my nose and chin as the magic took effect.

"Precisely," I said. "I want them all to see how shallow they are."

She shook her head.

"Go, then, imp. Play your tricks."

"I will." I hugged her and whisked the cloak around my shoulders once more.

"I will see you again soon, Mother Elspeth."

She swatted my backside as I fled out the door.

The sky had darkened considerably during my brief visit. I quickened my steps knowing my Father would only grow angrier the longer I delayed my arrival. Not that I meant to approach him while I looked like this.

I paused by a storefront and studied my reflection in the window. Elspeth's spell had given me a small hairy mole on my chin, added hair between my brows, and made my teeth and nose crooked. My brown eyes were still my own. I didn't look hideous, only plain and unnoticeable. I hoped it would be enough.

A scuff of noise and a soft chuckle had me whirling around. Two men stood on the opposite side of the narrow dirt path that this district called a road.

"Aren't you a pretty one?"

I groaned.

"Pretty? Please, sir. Plain is deserved at most."

His smile widened.

"Plain you might be, but you're a sight in that fancy dress with your haughty expression."

My jaw dropped.

"Haughty? You wound me twice."

"Bet you're worth a gold or two."

I snapped my mouth closed as I realized the precariousness of my situation. Father would not be pleased if these two attempted to ransom me. Not with my current appearance.

"Is that all men ever wonder? A woman's worth to them?" I asked as my mind raced for a solution.

The other man spoke up.

"No. I often wonder when I'll steal enough for a good drink and meal."

His companion laughed.

"Or when we'll find our next filly to fu—"

"Do you need assistance, miss?"

I turned my head toward the new voice on my right and watched a young man approach. He was dressed in clean clothes and well-groomed. While his appearance didn't state wealth, it certainly didn't shout questionable morals like the other two.

"She don't need nothing from the likes of you," one of my would-be abductors said.

The young man watched me, his light blue gaze holding mine as he waited for my response.

"I could use an escort if you please."

"Oh, we have that handled, love. We'll get 'ya where you need to be."

I took a step toward the young man, and the two men rushed toward me and grabbed my arms. The rank scent of stale beer and unwashed male assaulted my nose. The back of one man's hand brushed the side of my breast through my cloak and dress. I hoped he hadn't felt it. Yet, very real threads of panic wove through me, piercing my heart, lungs, and mind when it happened again. I struggled to think and breathe as my pulse hammered loudly in my ears.

"She's ours to escort, and the reward for her return ours to collect."

The young man exhaled heavily and began to remove his overcoat.

"If your intentions were true and fair, I would happily walk away. But we know they are not." He set the jacket aside on a swept doorstep.

"As they are not, we'll settle this with fists then."

While I appreciated the overture, two against one wasn't promising odds.

Think, Margaret. Think.

"You want to fight us?" One of my captors laughed.

"Afraid you might not win?" the young man taunted as he started to roll up his sleeves.

I glanced at the buildings. Weak glimmers of light shown through a few dirty glass panes. Calling for help might bring the residents forth, but in this area, would they be inclined to assist in freeing me or keeping me captive for coin?

Unsure, I kept my mouth closed and fisted my hands. Every lesson in sewing, etiquette, and dancing seemed useless in that moment. What I wouldn't have given for just one lesson in how to throw a decent punch.

I settled for stomping the wooden heel of my slipper onto the top of the man's foot to my right. He grunted and loosened his hold on me. The young man launched himself across the space separating us, his fist connecting with the jaw of the miscreant to my left. The hold on my arms loosened, and I wrenched myself free.

Grunts and sounds of flesh meeting flesh echoed behind me as I lifted my skirts and ran. I didn't go far. My gaze landed on a heavy metal pot that sat on someone's step. Hefting the weight, I gagged at the smell of feces and turned toward the fight once again.

The pair were working together, landing blow after blow on the young man's torso and arms. However, my rescuer was dispensing his own fists with determined precision. One of the men staggered back after a ringing jab to his head.

I lifted the metal container high as I rushed forward. The metal pot met the scoundrel's head with a resounding gong. The man crumbled to the ground with a slosh of dark liquid from the container I still gripped in my hands. Turning to the second rogue, I lifted my weapon, ready to assist, when the young man knocked the remaining man out with a square punch to his nose.

Without pause, my rescuer reached out and plucked the pot from my hands.

He stared at me for a long moment. In the dim light, while we both panted from our exertions, I noted the color of his blue eyes and the intensity of his regard. Something warm spread in my belly, and a blush ignited in my cheeks.

"I've never met a woman who used one of these as a bludgeon."

"I would have preferred not to as well," I said, averting my gaze and checking my hands. I'd avoided the slosh, unlike the unfortunate man at my feet, but still felt extremely dirty.

"There's a well not far from here if you would like to wash."

I looked up once more. Lingering wouldn't be prudent, yet I didn't want to leave.

"Please."

He set the pot aside and picked up his jacket. With the men no longer a threat, some of my reason returned. Enough to note the color of the young man's hair and the breadth of his shoulders.

"Thank you for your timely arrival," I said. "I don't know what I would have done without your assistance."

He smiled, a flash of white teeth.

"I have the feeling you would have managed something."

I returned his smile.

"My name is Margaret." I purposely omitted my last name, not wanting to influence his impression of me. He didn't even blink at my lack of formality.

"I'm Atwell," he said with a small bow.

Together, we walked down the darkened street.

"I apologize that you witnessed that," he said.

I glanced sideways at him.

"Apology not accepted. There's nothing to apologize for. That was the most excitement I've had in a long while." I paused. "That sounds horrible of me when you were the one being hit. Were you hurt?"

"A few bruises. Good reminders to move faster next time."

We arrived at the well, and he used the bucket to fetch me some water. While he poured it over my hands, I used a sliver of lye soap to scrub myself clean.

"I think that's everything," I said, looking down at myself.

When I met his gaze, I found him studying the bit of dress peeking from my cloak.

"You're far from home, aren't you?" he asked.

"A bit further than usual," I admitted. "I've been here before, though. However, never so late."

I dried my hands on the inside of my cloak, and when I was done, he offered his arm.

"Allow me to escort you home."

I accepted his arm.

"Not home. I'm expected somewhere else."

"Where?"

I hesitated to tell him. He would certainly recognize the name for what it was. A family of wealth.

"It's this way," I said instead.

He didn't comment on my evasiveness, and we walked in silence for several moments.

"It's already too late, isn't it?" I asked when he turned in the correct direction, escorting me back to the wealthier neighborhoods.

"Too late for what?"

"For you to base your opinion of me on my actions rather than where I live or my name."

"I most certainly am a man to weigh people based on their actions rather than their pocketbooks. However, I find it curious that you want me to do so. Most of your set prefer the opposite."

"I'm contrary like that," I said with a small laugh.

The road changed from trodden dirt to cobble, and I knew we were getting closer to my destination. My steps slowed. I looked at the flickering candles in the lanterns hung high on posts lining the street. I would be safe on my own now. Yet, I didn't loosen my hold on his arm, unwilling to give up the pleasant company for what awaited me.

"Do you often rescue damsels in the dark?" I asked.

Atwell chuckled.

"This was my first attempt. I'm not sure I would call it a success. I believe the damsel may have had a hand in the rescue."

I smiled, truly liking him. He wasn't boastful and didn't preen even though his looks warranted a bit of preening. His chiseled jaw and large biceps under my palm would be enough to make other girls of my position swoon. If both qualities belonged to someone with a name and wealth.

Why couldn't the boys my parents threw me at act more like Atwell?

A hint of music reached my ears, and I stopped walking altogether and faced Atwell.

"And does it bother you that someone of the gentler sex trounced her accoster?"

"Bother? Not at all. I'm intrigued and wish..." He shook his head. "I believe it would be best if you carry on without me from here. You should be safe enough."

I glanced down the lane. I couldn't yet see the three-story home that I knew waited, set back from the road and alit with candles, music, and unpleasant company. I wished I didn't have to go.

"Tell me what you wish," I said softly.

"It was a selfish thought."

That gained my undivided attention.

"Now you must tell me."

His gaze swept over my face before locking with my eyes.

"I would wish away your wealth so I might call on you in the morning. But in taking away your wealth, the wish would unmake you. And I like you just as you are." He caught my hand by the fingers and bent low over them.

"Take care, Margaret. And stay closer to home in the evenings."

He turned and left. For several long moments, I stared after him, wishing I had the power to grant his wish without changing me, because Atwell was more interesting than any boy I would find within the walls of the House of Greylin.

Squaring my shoulders, I faced my destination. A slow

smile lifted my lips as I imagined the reactions of the silly fops inside when they finally saw me.

That smile froze as I recalled my new imperfections.

Whirling, I faced the direction in which Atwell disappeared, and my mouth dropped open. He'd liked me while I was under a spell.

Atwell had truly liked me for me.

CHAPTER TWO

I STOOD IN THE STREET FOR A MOMENT BEFORE I started toward the house. My feet carried me forward as my mind raced. I had been so certain beauty and wealth were my only desirable attributes to a man. Atwell's interest in me, when he thought I had neither, had me doubting my thinking, and I wasn't sure how I felt about the new hope growing within me.

A marriage of love was unheard of by the wealthy in Towdown. Yet, I knew it existed. If not in the large homes near the castle, then elsewhere in the Kingdom of Drisdall. Even the king's marriage was said to be one of alliance rather than affection.

Despite knowing that, the small ball of hope continued to grow in my middle. I wasn't foolish enough to wish for love, but a common affection sounded lovely. I shook my head at the direction of my thoughts. Meeting one nice man did not mean I would walk into a room full of them. Yet, Atwell had proven that nice men did exist. Squaring my shoulders, I started up the drive.

Music and laughter poured from the open door. The attendant waiting to greet guests bowed to me as I approached.

"Margaret, House of Thoning," I said. "I need no announcement."

He nodded and bowed again as I entered the extravagant entry. Another servant waited near the cloakroom. I handed over the garment of questionable quality knowing she wouldn't comment, not when my dress fit the part of a wealthy Miss.

"Miss Thoning," I repeated so she would remember the correct cloak when I returned for it. Judith wouldn't be happy if I lost it.

Turning away, I studied the wide space divided lengthwise by stairs that led to the second and third floors. People walked from the parlor to the right and further back to the ballroom. To the left, I saw a long line of tables laden with finger food.

As tempting as it was to hide by the food, I knew I'd find the darling of this ball in the ballroom.

With demure steps and an averted gaze, I moved in that direction. No one paid much attention to me. Not in this crush of people. As soon as I reached the ballroom, warm air that bordered on stifling enveloped me.

I looked around, tapping my foot in time with the melody drifting from the strings of talented musicians. I loved music. However, the music and display of colorful silks never made up for the temperature or the company.

Dancers parted, and I caught a glimpse of Mother and Father speaking to Lord Greylin. I moved further into the throng of people encircling the room to avoid being seen.

On the surface, it appeared everyone was having a wonderful time. However, the Gentry of Drisdall always intermingled with questionable friendliness due to their never-ending pursuit for wealth and influence.

My gaze caught on Anthea and Aleese, who stood deep in conversation instead of dancing. Given the way they kept glancing at Brendal and his friends, I knew who they were discussing but not why. It seemed odd they were talking about him without Freshall.

Curious, I moved closer.

"I heard an agreement's already been made between the House of Thoning and Lord Greylin," Anthea, Freshall's closest friend said.

I felt a moment's panic. My parents wouldn't. Surely not.

"I cannot believe Lord Greylin would choose Margaret over Freshall. Freshall has a title," Aleese said.

"But little money."

It was precisely for that reason why, despite my best efforts, I was still sought after. The House of Thoning had money. Far too much of it. And as the only heir, that meant any family looking to gain wealth quickly showed interest in me. But only until their sons found the prospect of bedding me for a lifetime far too unappealing.

I looked over at Brendal, determined to do the same to him as I'd done to every prospect before him.

"But Brendal's father has substantial wealth," Aleese said. "Why would he...?"

Their conversation faded as I wove my way through the crowd toward where Brendal stood.

I'd long ago discovered the key to being noticed or ignored. It was all about one's presence. I walked meekly, shoulders curled in and head down a bit. No one minded me. Not even the cluster of boys laughing in a group near a set of open windows.

Taking a moment to enjoy the cool air, I waited.

"Hello, Brendal," I said softly, interrupting the banter with his friends.

The group turned to glance at me.

"Egad," Ashton said, a look of shock on his face as he stared at me.

"Is that you, Miss Thoning?" Horace, Aleese's older brother asked.

"Yes. I'm s-sorry about my ap-pearance," I said. "I didn't have t-time for a b-beauty s-s-spell."

I thought my stutter quite clever. None of these fops had spent more than a few required moments in my presence to actually know me.

Horace's gaze dipped to my middle.

"If having to choose between a pretty face or a trim waist, always choose the face," he said.

"I can't stop staring at her mole," Ashworth said in a mock whisper.

I couldn't have been more pleased with their reactions. Though I didn't let it show on my face. Turning toward Brendal, I gave him my full attention.

"My parents wanted me to introduce myself," I said with a small curtsy.

"Did they now?" He looked me over with a critical eye and shook his head. "You are homely at best. I suppose your figure isn't too bad. And you're right, a beauty spell could help the rest." He shrugged. "It isn't as if I have much choice in the matter."

He offered me his arm, and my mouth dropped open as my mind raced. I didn't want his bitter acceptance. I wanted his scorn and dismissal. An idea formed.

Accepting his arm, I let him escort me away from his friends.

"Y-you're wrong," I said.

"Oh, about what?"

"A s-s-spell helping. I a-always react b-badly. Horace saw the results of the last one. The w-weight I gained s-s-stayed with me for d-days after the s-s-spell wore off. The local caster s-said I should avoid all s-s-spells in the future."

He stopped walking and faced me.

"Please stop speaking," he said with an angry scowl. "It hurts to listen to you."

"It is obv-v-vious that you do not care for my presence. Sp-speak out against my p-presence, and my p-parents will listen."

"I most certainly will speak out against you. I find you repulsive and unpleasant to be near."

I struggled to keep the joy from my face. Thankfully, his gaze flicked to someone behind me so I could compose myself. When he looked at me once more, I had a suitably devastated expression upon my face.

"But it is not my decision to make," he said, killing my victory.

I angrily yanked my arm from his.

"Stubborn fool," I said crossly. "I will not suffer a lifetime of you."

He gave me an indolent shrug that made me want to stomp on his foot. Instead, turning to storm away, I crashed into a solid male chest.

"Father, Miss Thoning as requested," Brendal said from behind me.

I straightened away from the arms politely steadying me

and looked up at Lord Greylin. His bland expression didn't fool me, and I wondered how much he'd heard.

"Miss Thoning," he said with a nod and a sweeping glance at my face. "If you have a moment, I would like to speak with you privately."

"Of course," I said, already reaching for the arm he offered. A private discussion meant I could speak my mind without causing a scene. Hopefully, I would only need to point out Brendal's distaste for me for the matter of our nuptials to be settled. If not, I would flatly state I refused to wed him. The latter would upset my parents, but surely, they would see that having a title held no value to me.

Lord Greylin led me out of the ballroom to a study toward the back of his house. The small study was furnished comfortably with several chairs and a desk for the Lord to hand daily estate affairs.

"Please have a seat." He waited until I did so. "I apologize for Brendal's behavior. He will show you the respect required."

Those didn't sound like the words of a father willing to listen to reason. Quite the opposite. Desperate not to offend, yet equally desperate not to encourage, I chose my words carefully.

"Respect is necessary to keep a peaceful household," I said. "But it cannot be forced. Not true respect. That must be earned. And Brendal is too caught up in my appearance to ever consider truly respecting me."

Lord Greylin studied me for a long moment.

"While you may not have beauty, you do have a keen intelligence for someone your age. I admire that. I must admit that I found it odd that your father approached me, but I now understand why and am glad he did. We will be well suited for each other."

I stared at him not sure I was hearing correctly.

"We? You and I? Not Brendal and I?"

Lord Greylin smiled slightly. "Given Brendal's distaste for you, I think the pair of you would not have an easy life together. As it is, I'm prepared to place a condition on his inheritance to ensure he respects you appropriately. The condition will be easier to enforce once you're with child, of course."

His gaze swept over me, and I could see the hunger there. I took a hasty step back.

"I do not think we are suited," I said quickly.

"You do not wish to marry me?"

"What young miss would wish to marry a stranger?" Or a man the same age as her father, I thought to myself.

"I see. You wish to be courted."

"No, sir. I wish to be understood."

"And I wish to understand."

His words seemed sincere and gave me hope.

"I have parents who are determined to wed me to whomever holds the better advantage for our house. You say I have intelligence, and I say, 'what use is intelligence in chattel?' Do not misunderstand me. I do respect you, but I want to be more than a thing traded to bring more money to your household. I want to be valued for me. But how can any man value me when he does not know me?"

He tilted his head in acknowledgement, and I held my breath. Surely he would agree we could not wed.

"Then I will make an effort to know you between now and our wedding. Come. Let us return to the ballroom. I would like to speak to your father again."

Defeated for the moment, I took his arm and let him escort me from the study. Although I hadn't persuaded Lord Greylin to drop the matter, I still had the carriage ride home with my parents to make my feelings known. However, I couldn't let them see me until the spell wore off.

"Lord Greylin, I beg you continue without me," I said when we reached the ballroom. "I need a few moments to myself."

He nodded and released me with a polite bow. I curtsied in return then fled to the dining room. For the next hour, I nibbled and drank and avoided eye contact until my nose began to itch. Knowing the spell was finally wearing off, I went for my cloak.

The girl blinked at me when I said my name but didn't question me. When she handed me my cloak, I pressed a gold into her palm.

"For discretion and a message to my parents," I said.

She nodded.

"Can you let them know I'm not feeling well and am waiting for them in the carriage."

"Yes, ma'am."

While she scurried off, I went outside and looked for our carriage among those lined up along the drive.

As soon as our driver saw me, he hopped down from his position atop the carriage and helped me into my seat. I didn't know his name or ask it. Drivers, like most of our staff, didn't stay long. Father was concerned that they would figure out a way to steal from us. Most lasted a year. No more.

The practice of regularly dismissing one's servants was not limited to the House of Thoning. The gentry of Drisdall couldn't be bothered to care that the livelihood of others depended on them. They couldn't be bothered with more than their own petty—

The carriage door opened, startling me from my thoughts.

"There you are," Father said jovially. He offered his hand to Mother so she could step up into the carriage. Both of them smiled at me as they settled into their seats.

"Well done, Margaret," Father said, knocking on the top of the carriage.

With a small lurch, we started moving.

"I apologize for any inconvenience leaving early caused. I ate too much and am not feeling well," I said.

"Not at all, my dear."

Father's continued good humor worried me. He leaned back in the seat and patted Mother's hand.

"You must be so thrilled," she said. "I will admit I thought you would try to ruin this chance to wed Lord Greylin."

I stared at my mother, torn between anger and surprise that she believed I could be thrilled.

"Since I was under the impression you meant for me to meet the future Lord Greylin and not the present one, I cannot say I am thrilled."

"What then are you saying?" Father asked, his good humor fading. "Lord Greylin said you insisted on an extended engagement."

"Lord Greylin heard what he wished to hear." A trait men my father's age seemed to share.

"Speak plainly. Are you saying you do not wish to marry Lord Greylin, cousin to the king?" Father's face reddened as he spoke.

"What do you hope to gain from a union with Lord Greylin?" I asked.

"Audience with the King and Queen, of course," Mother said.

Father grunted his agreement.

"And will basking in their magnificence gratify you in some way? Do you think the populace will then bow and scrape to you, too?"

"Do not test me with your impertinence," Father said.

"Test you? I am merely trying to understand why you would sell me to a man twice my age. Or why a man twice my age, who already has wealth and an heir, would want me."

Father leaned forward. "I spoke to Lord Greylin because men your age will not have you. We are fortunate Lord Greylin will. As to his motives, I do not care."

"And that should be the basis of my agreement? Lord Greylin's benevolent tolerance of me? No. I refuse."

Father's face turned purple then white before assuming a hot red color that matched his coat.

"If you refuse this match, you will be cast from this house with no wealth or possessions, never to return."

I glanced at Mother. Her hands were tightly clenched and her eyes downcast.

I opened my mouth to say more, but a bang on the roof interrupted me. The carriage started to slow. A shout rang out above the sound of the carriage wheels over cobble.

Father switched to my seat and opened the sliding panel in the wall that showed the view ahead of us. The low hum of more voices briefly filled the carriage before Father closed the panel once more.

"Something is afoot," Father said. "Stay inside."

He opened the door and left me alone with Mother.

"And will you throw me away so easily?" I asked softly.

"If you carry so little affection for your family, then I must."

"How does marrying Lord Greylin show my affection for you and Father?"

"It is our way into the castle. Your Father's way to cultivate a relationship with the people who can grant the permission he needs to establish larger trade routes."

"You're selling me to gain more wealth?"

"We are not selling you."

"How large of a dowry is Lord Greylin receiving?"

Mother had the grace to flush and look away.

Outside the carriage, the wail of crying joined the shouts. Before I could open the panel to see what was happening, the door opened, and Father entered.

"Perilous times," he said quietly as he took his seat and banged on the roof.

"What is it?" Mother asked with concern.

"The Queen of Turre is dead."

"Childbirth?" Mother asked. "Five pregnancies can put a strain on—"

"It was not childbirth that killed the queen. Those sharing the news speculate it was magic."

"And the king? Does he live? His heirs?"

"Of that there was no news." He thoughtfully tapped his thigh. "This could change things. At best, trade will slow because the royal family is in mourning."

"And the worst that might happen?" Mother asked.

"Turre might cast its accusing gaze at Drisdall and shut down trades completely." His gaze locked with mine. "I cannot risk the future of our House on the whimsies of a child. Tomorrow I will send word to Lord Greylin. You shall be married within fourteen days."

My stomach twisted.

"How can a long engagement possibly cause our family to fall to ruin?"

"We need to establish secondary trade routes to prepare for the worst. I will discuss this no further."

I set my hands demurely on my lap.

"As you say, Father."

The carriage continued its rocking journey home. The low murmur of voices and shouts faded while silence reigned inside.

What more was there to say? Father's determination to marry me to a man that I did not know, remained firm. Yet, I would not consent to wed a stranger twice my age only to appease my Father's fears of the future. If he would not accept my spoken refusal, he left me no choice but to act.

A cold fear filled my belly, but it did not sway me from my decision. Father had been clear what would happen if I refused. I would be cast aside. Disowned.

I turned my head and peeked through the carriage curtains. People moved along the edges of the cobbled lanes. I knew how dangerous it could be out there. But Atwell had shown me that not all men are cut from the same tattered cloth; and the terrifying uncertainty of leaving home filled me with less dread than the thought of marrying Lord Greylin.

Leaning back into my seat, I accepted the single suitable course of action left to me.

Tomorrow, I would run.

CHAPTER THREE

THE MULTITUDE OF SKIRTS TANGLED AROUND MY LEGS. If not for the slow, quiet pace I maintained, I would have fallen head first down the stairs.

The first light of the new day dimly lit the narrow back hall leading from the stairs to the back of the house. With a lumpy bag at my back and the volume of skirts from three layered dresses, I barely fit.

Each brush of fabric against the wall made me cringe with the certainty that someone would hear. However, as I neared the kitchen, I knew I needn't worry. The soft clink and scrape of pottery and pan covered any sound I made as the cook and Judith prepared the morning meal.

I waited in the entry to the kitchen, listening to the familiar sounds and picturing what the cook and Judith were doing. It was a routine I'd witnessed often enough. The cook at the butcher board. Judith either at the pot or gathering dishes to set the table. Occasionally even fetching items from the cold storage. That's what I waited for. When she left her post, the cook would have her back to the entry to stir the pot, and I would be able to slip out the door.

A scrape of noise sounded behind me on the stairs. My eyes widened at my carelessness. I hadn't considered the housemaids. Panicking, I peeked into the kitchen. Both Judith and the cook had their backs to me. Easing the door open, I slipped outside.

Dawn's early light created dusky shadows over the yard. The chickens and goats moved in their pens back by the stables. Everything else remained quiet.

With determined steps, I walked away from the only life I knew. Armed with the ornate dresses I wore and the meager possessions in my bag, I struck out on a new path. One I felt certain would lead to a happier life.

Very few people moved about this early among the big houses near the castle. As I walked, I noted a horse and guard leaving the castle grounds through a side gate. I envied his ease of travel but knew leaving on foot was the safer option for a quiet escape.

The gentle clop of the horse's hooves faded as the rider gained distance. I followed in his wake toward the Market district. There, people moved about, setting up their tables for the day to display their wares.

One farmer had already unloaded produce. As I walk past, I heard him direct his son to take the wagon to the stables further from the Market where it would not hinder prospective customers. I knew of a stable not far from Elspeth and followed the young man. When the wagon slowly rumbled forward, I nimbly hopped on the back. He never noticed my company, and I made better time than walking.

When the wagon brought me near Elspeth's as I'd hoped, I left the wagon and strode toward Elspeth's humble cottage. Her comments about feeling like my mother would be tested in the next moments. And though my own mother had sat in silence as my father threatened to disown me, I hoped that Elspeth would be more than a mother figure. I desperately needed a friend too. For, if she chose to turn me away, I had nowhere else to go. I thought of the years I'd been going to Elspeth for spells. Since I was old enough to understand what a spell meant. Freedom. And freedom was exactly what I sought now. She would understand. She had to.

I turned the corner and spotted a familiar horse standing in front of Elspeth's home. My steps slowed. The guard from earlier was now cloaked and spoke to Elspeth by the door. The low murmur of his voice barely graced the early morning silence, and I wondered what a castle guard needed of a caster. A love spell perhaps?

The guard straightened and turned my way, having heard my approach. With a small bow to me, he moved back to his horse, got on, and started down the opposite end of the street.

Elspeth opened her mouth, clearly ready to scold my early visit. However, her gaze caught on the bag I carried, and her disapproving expression changed to worry.

She waited until I was inside her home and the door firmly closed before questioning me.

"What brings you here so early? And with so much clothing?"

"Mother and Father gave me a choice. Wed Lord Greylin—the current Lord—or become disowned. I chose the latter and left before they woke."

"Margaret, it is not uncommon to marry—"

"Do not tell me I should consider marrying a man old enough to have fathered me. While others may think it's suitable, I do not. You know I would be miserable."

"Do I? I have met Lord Greylin. He is a decent man. As kind as any man in his position is."

"Which says nothing about his character. I've yet to meet someone with wealth who doesn't turn a blind eye to the people struggling to eat every day. The people you help with what you earn. You, who has very little. How can we excuse those with wealth for taking no action?" My righteous deflection fell on knowing, deaf ears.

"That is not why you do not want to wed him."

"I do not want to wed him because he said a spell could fix my beauty."

"He thinks you too beautiful?"

"Recall that he saw me under the influence of a spell to rob me of my beauty. I thought the chin wart magnificent, by the way."

"I see. So, you ran from home. What do you intend, Margaret?"

"You have no apprentice. I have watched you make potions since I was this high." I held up my hand. "I already know much of your trade."

"Your parents will regret their decision and come back for you within days."

"Not if they never learn where I am. Please, Elspeth. I have nowhere else to go and refuse to be auctioned off like a mare for breeding."

She gave an exasperated sigh and shook her head at me.

"As if I would ever turn you away, imp. Remove some of those layers while I search for a bag. I hope you are not fond of those dresses. If you truly mean to disappear, we will need to get rid of them."

"I was thinking we could sell them for something plainer. And perhaps trade for a cloak more suited for this area."

She looked at my cloak critically, checking the thick lining.

"This is modest, but anyone with an eye would know it's more than anyone here could afford. We'll take this with us."

"Take? Where?"

"I need to go to the Brazen Belle for some information and supplies."

My brows rose, and she laughed at me.

"Reconsidering being my apprentice?"

"I'm only curious what business we have there and why you think they are suited to sell my dresses."

"Men don't always have coin. Sometimes it's easier to trade a wife's pretty gown. No one raises an eye when a whore trades a pretty dress for coin."

She watched me closely when she used the word "whore."

"You're not trying to scare me away by visiting a place you think I won't like, are you? Because it won't work. I will go anywhere I must."

"I'm not trying to scare you. I have business there."

"We have business there." She smiled at my inclusion. "Does this business have to do with the guard I saw? Does he fancy someone at the Brazen Belle?"

"It would be much simpler if he did. Unfortunately, it is something much more complex that I need from the Brazen Belle. We'll speak of this more when we return. Hurry now."

Within minutes, we set out at a brisk pace. The streets were no longer as quiet as before. People moved about their business, starting their day. No one paid us much attention.

Elspeth carried my spare dresses in a bundle. I struggled

to keep up. My stomach rumbled, begging for breakfast. I ignored it. Elspeth did not.

"They will have something for us in the kitchen there."

I made no comment, unsure what to expect from a whorehouse meal. While I knew everyone needed to do what they must to eat, I couldn't help but wonder what would make a woman choose prostitution over marriage. At least with marriage, a woman only needed to sleep with one man, as distasteful as he might be.

In the distance, I could hear the din from the Market district. Vendors shouting their wares. Conversations overlapping one another. The clatter of footsteps over the cobble. I could also smell the delicious aromas of freshly cooked foods and pastries. I loved mornings in the Market. And some large part of me reveled in the fact that I would be able to spend more time there now.

The Brazen Belle stood out among the other businesses on its narrow dirt path. Taller than its neighbors, the lower half of the establishment was a bawdy bar room where wenches wore questionable dresses that barely contained their bosoms. Even at this early hour, there were patrons waiting for ale and perhaps a little cuddle from the serving women once the libation had been delivered.

One of the women, walking the room with a tray laden with mugs, spotted Elspeth and winked at us. Elspeth nodded in return and steered me toward the kitchen. In the back, the cooks were busily preparing the day's stew and baking their own bread. Elspeth sat me down at the table and asked them to feed me.

"Don't you want me to accompany you?" I asked when she turned to leave.

"Not this time. I think we will slowly ease you into everything the Brazen Belle has to offer."

A few of the kitchen staff snickered, and Elspeth gave them a censoring look.

"Take care of my new apprentice. See that no one bothers her."

They both nodded quickly.

Satisfied, Elspeth took my cloak and dresses, except for the one I wore, and left me in the warmth of the kitchen. One of the kitchen maids placed a bowl before me, and I quietly ate the stew. It wasn't as tasty as what came from Mother and Father's kitchens. But I didn't mind.

I'd barely scraped the bottom when Elspeth returned. The bundle of dresses was gone, and in its place was a bag that cast a soft blue glow at its seams.

"It is time to go, Margaret. We have much to do."

Excitement filled me as I realized that this time I would be the one helping create the magic. I wondered what kind.

I WIPED the sweat from my brow then switched hands to ease the ache in my right arm.

"Don't stop," Elspeth warned yet again.

"After two days, I understand what 'keep stirring' means, Elspeth."

I stared at the muck in the pot. The soft blue glow of the three moonflowers had faded as soon as the spring water first boiled. The rank smell had grown with each ingredient Elspeth added to the pot at regular intervals.

"Do you think it's true?" I asked.

"The news about Turre?"

"Yes. There's been nothing since the night before I arrived. The king's emissaries should have returned with news."

"Not necessarily," Elspeth said. "It takes a fair number of days for most merchants to cross through the Dark Forest."

I thought of the extensive swath of woods that separated the two kingdoms of Turre and Drisdall. Even with the enchanted passage that protected travelers from the creatures that prowled the shadows, not many willingly ventured the route. Those who did, did so with haste.

"But, merchants with heavily laden loads are slower than men with swift mounts," I said. "Something must have delayed the king's men."

"Likely waiting for an audience with a grieving king. Focus on the potion."

I continued to stir, staring into the pot, watching for the moment the mixture turned a color. What color, I did not know. However, I did understand what we were making. Elspeth had explained it to me the moment we had returned from the Brazen Belle.

The guard I'd noted the morning of my arrival had been sent on behalf of the royal family of Drisdall who feared an attack like the one the royal family of Turre was rumored to have endured. The queen had requested a means of defending her family against magical attack. The potion I stirred was only one part of creating protective amulets for the king, queen, and their small son.

"I can't decide if I should find it comforting that there are parents who still care so much about their child or if I should find the king and queen entirely selfish for only thinking of their family and not the rest of the Kingdom." It didn't matter that protecting the kingdom was beyond Elspeth's skill or any other caster in existence—the great casters who'd fought in the great war now long gone. The request seemed entirely too selfish.

"Do try to keep those thoughts to yourself when we meet the royal family. I rather like having my head upon my shoulders."

I turned to look at Elspeth who was carving oval disks from Elder, Ash, and Oak.

"I'm going to meet the royal family?"

"Of course. You are my apprentice."

I grinned and turned back to the pot. If my mother and father knew I was to have an audience with the king and queen before they could, they would be positively green with envy.

"As for how to think of the king and queen," Elspeth said. "Think well of them as the king and queen are fair rulers, and by preserving their lives, they are ensuring our way of life."

"But should our way of life be preserved?" I asked, thinking of Mother and Father and others of the gentry.

"There is poverty and injustice everywhere, Margaret. Changing rulers will not change that. Look at the good that exists because of our current rulers."

"You're right. It's not the king or queen's fault that their wealthy subjects are selfish, braying asses."

Elspeth snorted.

"I hope you can channel that passion into potions. We could use the wealth to better the lives of those around us."

I grinned and focused on my task.

"You're right. I should not place the fault of others on those in charge. No one can choose how I should behave except me. The same holds true for everyone else."

A swirl of yellow suddenly burst forth in the pot, and I quickly used the coarse skirts of my newly acquired dress to remove the boiling mixture from the flames.

"What color did you see?" Elspeth asked.

"Yellow," I said.

"Very good. Set it on the stool, and continue stirring until it changes again."

Elspeth and I continued our idle conversations covering whatever topic struck my fancy. Over the past two days, I had yet to grow tired of her company or she mine. It made the endless hours of work easier and more enjoyable.

As if reading my mind, she asked, "Any second thoughts about apprenticing with me?"

"Not one."

The yellow faded from the muck in the pot.

"The color is gone," I said, looking at her with concern.

"It happens. Or so I've been told. Keep stirring."

I switched arms again.

"After I'm done with this piece, we will trade places," she said. "I need you to pick up the flattened gold from the blacksmith."

I was more than ready to escape the monotony of pot-stirring.

"I'll buy us both meat pies on the way back."

In less than an hour, I was walking the dirt paths toward the Market district. With the large hood of my very plain cloak tugged low over my brow, I wasn't concerned about anyone recognizing me. I wasn't dressed well enough to be recognized. And for once, I was grateful for the snobbery of the gentry.

Stretching my legs with long, brisk strides, I inhaled deeply of the clean, crisp air. It was good to escape the smoke-filled cottage. However, I felt certain that the smell of the concoction still clung to me.

Near the Market district, I spotted a face I thought never to see again. Atwell was speaking to the very blacksmith I needed to approach. A smile curved my lips.

"I'm sorry, son," I overheard the blacksmith say. "I haven't seen him since he left. The wheels were good. The axle as well. If he's delayed, I don't believe it's because of wagon trouble."

Atwell's shoulders sagged.

I cleared my throat lightly, hoping to improve his mood, and the pair looked at me.

"Hello again, Mister Smith," I said with a bright smile. "I'm here to collect the discs for Elspeth."

"I told you, miss. It's just Smithy or Randall, whichever you prefer."

"Thank you, Randall."

He walked away to fetch my order, and I looked at Atwell.

"Hello again," I said.

He frowned slightly and gave the barest of bows.

"Forgive me, miss. Do I know you?"

"You probably don't recognize me." I lowered my voice and stepped closer. "My appearance was a bit different the last time we met. If you recall, I used a chamber pot to bash someone over the head."

Recognition lit his eyes, and his gaze swept over my face again.

"Margaret?" He didn't look like he believed it was me.

"Yes. The true Margaret. I apologize for how I looked before."

He frowned.

"No, I apologize. I don't have time for childish games. Excuse me."

He moved to step away, and I caught his arm. He immediately stopped and looked down at me.

"It wasn't a game," I said quickly. "It was a desperate attempt to save myself from something I didn't want. I am truly sorry if I offended you."

Some of the annoyance faded from his expression.

"Not offended. It is good to see you again, Margaret, however I really must go. I'm looking for my father."

I nodded and released him.

"Perhaps we'll see each other again soon."

With more than a little regret, I watched him walk away.

The blacksmith returned with flattened discs so thin one bent in the palm of my hand.

"Thank you, Randall," I said.

With the gold protectively wrapped in a piece of leather, I started back for the cottage, but not before I grabbed our meat pies. Mine didn't make the journey home. I was too hungry, and the little meal was too warm to resist. Because it was already finished, I was able to take over the stirring the moment I walked in the door.

"I can't believe how thin he managed to pound this gold," Elspeth said, inspecting what I had brought back.

"Given that you told him he could keep any remaining gold, I'm sure he spent time pounding it as thin as he could manage."

As I started stirring, I watched Elspeth layer the gold between the discs of wood. When she was done she wound the layers in twine until three ovals dangled from separate strings she tied to a single twig.

"It looks like you're going to make candles."

"It does. However, once we dip these into the potion, they should come out looking nothing like they do now."

I studied the three wooden discs now covered in twine and wondered what exactly they would look like when she was finished.

It took several hours more before the potion turned a vibrant green. I stopped stirring, and Elspeth immediately dipped the twine balls into the mixture. Together, we chanted the words she'd made me practice repeatedly over the last two days.

"Elder to gold, protect and hold. Gold to Ash, glow bright and flash. Ash to gold, magic controlled. Gold to oak, hide and cloak. To twine wrapped round and round, all magic shall rebound."

The potion, which had long ago cooled, began boiling anew, and a bright flash of blue light filled the room. When I could see once more, the pot was empty except for three glittering, green ovals, each the size of a gold piece. If a gold piece were oval shaped.

"Did they turn to emeralds?" I asked as Elspeth lifted one.

"No. Stones of protection. Hold this." She set one in my palm and immediately slapped me.

"Ow! Why did you do that?"

"A test."

"Of my patience or my complexion?"

"Of the stone." She moved away and grabbed one of her pre-made vials. "Hold still."

Before I could object, she threw the vial at my feet. A dark mist rose up, and the stone in my palm glowed brightly.

"Do you feel anything?" Elspeth asked.

"No. What should I feel?"

"Nothing if the stone is working. If it's not working, incredible pain eating its way up your legs."

I looked at the glowing stone. Green lights whirled within the green orb.

"It seems to be working," Elspeth said. "Grab your cloak. It's time for us to meet the king and queen."

CHAPTER FOUR

WE APPROACHED A SIDE GATE GUARDED BY TWO cloaked men. Listening to the direction of the guard who'd visited Elspeth, she and I had our hoods down low, covering as much of our faces as we could. When we reached the guards, Elspeth spoke first.

"I'm Elspeth, a magic caster, summoned by the queen."

"And who is she?" the guard asked nodding to me.

"My apprentice."

The man nodded and motioned us inside. Another guard escorted us around to a gated entrance. We never saw any servants or prettily dressed people once we were through the gate, which was how I'd imagined life in the castle. Instead, it was just the guard who escorted us down a narrow hall and up several staircases.

The guard stopped in front of a very plain door in the middle of one of the narrow hallways. I glanced at Elspeth, wondering why we were in what appeared to be a servant's wing. Had she misunderstood who we would be meeting?

The man rapped sharply twice on the wood panel then turned to us.

"Stay here until you're summoned."

As soon as he disappeared from sight, Elspeth looked at me.

"Remember your place. You're an apprentice. You'll be in the presence of the queen and king. Do not speak unless I give you permission. Do you understand?"

"Do you really think we'll meet the queen? This doesn't seem very queenly," I said with a quick glance at the hall.

"Our type will never see the main halls, imp. It's the servants' entrance for us. Always."

Understanding and a little awe dawned as I nodded, trying to suppress my giddy excitement. It wasn't every day a person met royalty. Some waited lifetimes without even sighting anyone wearing a crown. Yet here I was, not only about to see our kingdom's rulers but to hear them speak. Possibly have a conversation with them. It didn't matter if I was entering through the servants' entrance or not.

"What is going through that mind of yours? Spit it out quickly."

"It's nothing but excitement. I won't speak. I know my place."

We didn't wait too long before the door opened, and a maid bade us to enter.

I wasn't sure what I was expecting to walk into, but it wasn't the bedroom in which we found ourselves. Although the large bed was hung with heavy drapes and silks, ornately decorated with embroidered leaves and stags, and the rich creams, golds, and greens made it seem a forest bed from fairy tales, it was still a bedroom. Did the king and queen often entertain in their sleeping chambers?

Pulling my gaze from the bed, I quickly considered the rest of the room. There wasn't anything in the room to suggest it was a common place to greet guests.

"Her Majesty cannot be bothered with charlatans and false promises," the woman said, drawing my attention. "You can demonstrate to me whatever trinket or potion you think you have that will help."

Ignoring the woman's abrupt attitude, I looked at Elspeth. Another demonstration didn't bode well for me. My cheek still felt a little tender.

"I have three amulets to protect against magical influences." Elspeth withdrew the amulets from her cloak along with three vials.

"These vials are potions meant to cause the victim pain. When thrown to the ground, anyone in the vicinity will become affected. I do not sell these. They are far too dangerous."

She held out her hands, offering the vials to the maid.

"Choose which one of us should wear an amulet and which one should go without so you can see the results."

I looked sharply at Elspeth.

"Your friend doesn't seem to like your idea," the maid said noting my look.

"My apprentice helped test an amulet before arriving," Elspeth said. "She wasn't prepared for the unexpected pain."

I frowned at Elspeth. She was making it sound like she had used a vial on me when in fact all she'd done was slap me. Every word she said was true though. I hadn't been prepared for the sudden slap.

"I see," the woman said. "Your apprentice can wear an amulet, then."

Elspeth handed me an amulet, and I took it reluctantly. As much as I wanted to be the courageous pupil and refuse to spare her pain, she'd purposely done what she had in the cottage to ensure I'd wear the protection. And there had to be a good reason for that.

"Make sure the amulet is touching your skin," she said.

I put the charm around my neck so the maid could see it while still allowing the stone to touch me. Without warning, the woman threw a vial at our feet. A white vapor rose, crawling up our skirts. On my chest the amulet began to glow blue.

Elspeth cried out and fell to her knees while I felt nothing. And, it wasn't just pain she was feeling. Red marks appeared on her skin, visual proof she wasn't faking.

The maid took a few hasty steps back and watched us as

Elspeth continued to writhe and make horrible pained sounds.

Unable to bare another moment, I leaned forward to try to help Elspeth. The amulet fell forward, breaking contact with my skin. The mist felt like a thousand coals being racked over my skin. With a strangled cry, I straightened. A hint of red dotted the skin along my arms.

Standing straight, I used my skirts to fan the vapors. It took several moments for the mist to clear. Even once it cleared, Elspeth continued to breathe shallowly. Her skin was mottled with blisters and deep, angry burns.

The maid clapped her hands loudly and several of the doors leading to the room opened.

"Fetch these women chairs and something to eat and drink," the maid commanded.

Several of the maids who entered curtsied deeply and bowed their heads. With a sinking feeling, I looked at the woman before us again.

I had done what I had resented so many of my class for doing. I had judged the woman based on how she was dressed. I should have known to look deeper. Her rigid posture. Her regal demeanor. We had just been tested by the queen.

"How long will the effects of that vial last?" she asked.

Elspeth struggled to stand, and I hurried to help her up. She hissed when my hand came in contact with a burn on her palm.

Once she was standing, she answered the queen.

"Until I heal, Your Majesty."

The queen looked down at the two vials in her hand.

"Why bring three vials?"

"I made three amulets. Three vials to test each."

I looked at Elspeth in shock. She couldn't endure more vials.

The queen seemed to think the same.

"I think it is unnecessary for you to endure another vial. Perhaps your apprentice?"

I'd had a taste of the pain and knew it wouldn't be easy. But I couldn't allow Elspeth to endure another vial. I nodded my acceptance to the queen even as Elspeth shook her head.

"I will endure," Elspeth said.

"I rather believe you would," the queen said.

The maids returned with chairs, and I helped Elspeth sit. Once she was comfortable, and the queen was seated, the questions began.

"Tell me how the charms work," she said. "And be sure to include all the cautions and pitfalls."

Elspeth lifted her hand and gestured at me.

"Speak for me until I catch my breath," she said.

Although Elspeth had spent the last several days teaching me about the amulets we made, and I was more than capable of repeating that information, it worried me that she deferred to me. Her continued shallow breathing told me of her pain. We needed to return to the cottage so I could care for her. There was a salve she made that could help ease the pain from the burns.

Knowing her suffering would remain until the queen was satisfied, I spoke quickly.

"The stone protects against all magic, good and bad. If you try to use a spell to enhance your beauty, it won't work," I said bluntly with another quick glance at Elspeth. She didn't even look like she cared what I was saying, a true indication of just how much pain she was enduring.

"Do you have any willow bark tea? It might help Elspeth."

"My maids will bring something for her shortly. Please continue."

"As you saw, in order for its protection to work, it must be touching your skin. The stone itself is fragile and should be protected. Although it works against magic, non-magical means can still hurt you and destroy it. A direct blow could crack the stone and end its protection."

"If I wear it against my skin, inside my bodice to maintain contact, how will I know when magic is being used against me?"

"There is no way, other than the glow, to know when magic is being used against you."

"I see. It makes it hard to identify if someone is trying to hurt us when we don't know when we're being hurt."

"The stone is designed for protection. It is not meant to tell you when someone is trying to hurt you."

"Margaret," Elspeth said sharply. "Recall to whom you are speaking.

"I'm sorry, Your Majesty."

"Don't apologize," the queen said. "You're speaking truthfully, and I appreciate your honesty. With what is happening in Turre, I'm trying to prepare for the same. Now, will the magic in the stone wear out?"

"No. Each amulet was made with a moonflower. It will endure any magic so long as the stone remains unbroken."

"Any magic made," Elspeth said. "However, it can only endure a limited amount of blood magic."

"Blood magic?" the queen asked.

I took over the explanation as this part of magical lore had interested me from the moment I'd learned of it years ago.

"Magic is nothing but a person's attunement with their surroundings and their ability to manipulate the energy in every living thing. Every man, woman, and child is born with a certain amount of ability. The majority of us have the barest trace and are unable to do any magic. Those who can are considered casters. Some casters have more ability; others have less.

"While rare among the people, casters are the most common type of person to use magic. The less common are those who have more than an attunement with their environment. They don't just manipulate the energy around them; they share it. The very energy of everything around them is in their blood. We call those enchanters. It's extremely rare."

"I don't understand why the stone would deflect endless caster magic but only limited blood magic," the queen said.

"Because the amount of magic a caster can send your way is limited. A caster can be exhausted, which disrupts the attunement with their source of energy. An enchanter is connected to their source of energy, and because of that, they will not tire."

"You need not worry about blood magic, though," Elspeth said.

A door opened, and maids walked in. We stopped speaking as they served Elspeth some tea. My mentor drank greedily and remained silent until the doors closed once more.

"Why do you think I shouldn't worry about blood magic?" the queen asked.

"The use of blood magic cannot be hidden," Elspeth said. "It will perverse the environment. It will cause changes that will be noticeable by all. The Dark Forest is a good example of what happens with the use of blood magic. Too much energy was drawn from the area. The plants and creatures are no longer the same."

The queen nodded slowly, and I thought of the woods they mentioned. Running from the mountains several weeks' ride to the north, to the waters to the south, the swath of trees completely separated the two kingdoms. Unnatural, deadly creatures called the Dark Forest home, and I was glad for the barrier that kept them there.

"The forest was created centuries ago, during the wars," the queen said.

"Precisely," Elspeth said.

The queen continued to quiz us for another hour. When she seemed satisfied with the answers, she slipped one of the amulets around her neck.

"I will allow you to take your mentor home to rest. But I ask that you return as soon as she's fit. I will have more questions by then."

Elspeth paused on the dirt path. It was well after midnight, and our journey home had taken far longer than anticipated.

"Is that someone in front of my door?" she asked.

I peered toward her cottage, trying to see through the gloom. A large, dark shape unfurled from the ground near the door. It took a moment for me to discern arms and legs.

"Your eyes are better than mine," I said. "It does look like a man."

Elspeth straightened and started walking toward her home.

After my late-night run in with the two men several nights ago, I was more hesitant to greet a faceless shape in the dark. However, when I saw the face, I couldn't help but smile.

"Atwell? What are you doing here?" I asked.

"I need help." He looked at Elspeth. "I know you do spells. Can you help me locate my father?"

I frowned, not because I didn't want to help him but because I wasn't sure Elspeth could. Not in her current condition.

"Come inside," I said, opening the door for both of them. "We can discuss this by the fire."

It took me a few moments to rekindle a flame in the hearth. Once a cozy heat emanated, I started brewing Elspeth some more tea to help with the pain and the healing.

"Why do you need to find your father?" Elspeth asked when she'd caught her breath again.

"Before news came from Turre, my father left with a supply laden wagon. He trades there once a month. It usually takes him four days. He's been gone eight. Nine now," Atwell said, looking at the dark window. "It's not like him to be this late, and with the news..."

He needn't say more. Many people were speculating things about the current state of Turre. Since the news of the queen's death, no one had come from the passage through the Dark Forest.

"Do you have something of his. Something personal?" Elspeth asked.

"Just myself," Atwell said.

"Does your father love you very much?"

"He does."

"Very well. Margaret, I will need you to prepare everything."

I handed her the tea to sip and followed every instruction she gave me. When it came to saying any words, I brought the bowl to her.

"When I'm finished, the water will show us Turre, Drisdall, and the path between. If your father is anywhere within those boundaries, we will see a spark of light in the water."

She spoke a few words, and the water began to shimmer in the bowl. A mist rose in two places. One cleared, and I saw the symbol of the House of Drisdall. The other remained murky. Between the two, a very small speck of green light moved in minute, unpredictable twitches.

"He is alive, and it looks like he is slowly making his way to Drisdall." She frowned and studied the water some more. "I don't believe he is with a wagon. A horse perhaps? His movement is too erratic."

She sat back as the magic faded.

"I know this is hard to hear, but be patient. Do not go into the passage to look for him. Too many have gone in and not returned in recent days. Your father is a strong, intelligent man. If he loves you as much as you say, he will find a way home to you."

Atwell nodded.

Elspeth closed her eyes with a sigh, and I motioned Atwell to the door. I waited until we were outside to speak.

"I'm sorry the news wasn't better."

"It was more than I had before."

I reached out and clasped his hand. He looked down at it for a long moment.

"Why did you use a spell to make yourself different if not for a prank?"

"My name is Margaret," I said softly, "of the House of Thoning. That night, my parents wanted me to meet someone important. A marriage prospect. A man twice my age who has no interest in who I am but only the poise I possess and the quiet intellect to go with it. The spell was a test of his character. He failed."

I met Atwell's steady gaze.

"But you did not. You came to my rescue and spoke to me civilly, despite my appearance."

"A wart and crooked teeth couldn't hide your beauty, Margaret. I'm surprised this man didn't see the same thing I did."

I smiled slightly. "Many people are blind."

He squeezed my fingers gently then released me.

"What do I owe for the spell?"

I waved away his question. "Go home; wait for your father. I hope he returns to you soon."

He nodded and turned to leave. After only a few steps, he paused and looked back at me.

"Can I call on you tomorrow?"

I smiled widely.

"I would like that very much."

I could barely contain my squeal when I went back inside. Elspeth, who had had her eyes closed, now watched me with speculation.

"Well, out with it. What happened that put such color in your cheeks?"

"Atwell asked if he could see me tomorrow."

Elspeth sighed. "For all your fascination with magic, I knew it would never last. Which is just as well because you don't have much ability my dear. You're good for stirring, though."

I grinned.

The next morning dawned bright, and I dressed quickly, excited for the new day. Quietly making my way down the ladder from the loft space above the kitchen, I saw Elspeth still lay in bed, an indication that she continued to feel the pain from the spell.

It would be hours yet before anyone would call on Elspeth. Or me. To keep myself busy, I decided Elspeth could use a long soak in some healing salts. With a bit of effort, I managed to drag the large copper bathing tub near the fire and began the arduous process of filling it for her. She roused as I poured the last pot of steaming water in.

To give her privacy and some peace, I left to visit the Market district. My mind kept returning to thoughts of Atwell along the way. I wondered what time he might arrive. If he'd heard from his father yet. What kind of meals he preferred. I shook my head at myself and focused on the task at hand.

I wanted to buy some fresh bread with some of the coin the queen had given us. Although I knew much of the coin would go to helping others, I didn't think Elspeth would mind a hot breakfast.

However, when I reached the Market district, there wasn't the usual bustle and din of voices. People spoke in hushed tones, and there were far fewer of them.

I went straight to the baker.

"A loaf of bread and news," I said, laying five coppers on his counter.

"There are rumors that some of the folk living in the outskirts have gone missing," he said, collecting the coins and setting a loaf on the counter. "Just disappeared. Overnight. No one saw or heard anything."

I nodded, took my bread home, and shared the news with Elspeth as she dried her hair by the fire.

"It's not the first time folks near the woods have disappeared," she said.

I dabbed cream on the burns on her back and handed it to her so she could do her legs.

"When folk disappear, the magic creating the barrier to protect us needs to be strengthened. I'm sure the king and queen will send someone out to test it today."

Her words reassured me until sometime later when I answered a sudden knock on the door and saw a guard there.

"The queen summons you."

It took longer to reach the queen this time because of the sores on Elspeth's feet. The guard didn't offer his horse along the way, and my friend leaned on me heavily the entire time.

"We should have said no," I said under my breath as we slowly made our way up the final flight of stairs.

"You know better," Elspeth panted. "One does not refuse the queen."

This time when the guard knocked, the door swung open immediately.

"Come," the queen said, stepping aside. She was dressed in a similar fashion as the day before. A plain dress with a simple hair style.

As I guided Elspeth to the waiting chair, I wondered if

the queen dressed plainly to confuse people or if she preferred it.

Elspeth refused to sit. Instead, she watched the queen pace in agitation.

"Is something wrong with the amulets, Your Majesty?" Elspeth asked when the queen remained quiet.

The queen abruptly stopped pacing and faced us.

"The amulets seem to be fine. Have you heard news of people going missing?"

"We had heard such news," Elspeth said. "It has been known to happen when the magic holding back the beasts of the Dark Forest weakens."

"We sent someone to check the strength this morning. The wards are fine. I believe it is something more than a simple magical enhancement. Not only are people from the outskirts missing, I've heard that children from our Houses are missing as well. A girl from the House of Thoning has been missing for days."

CHAPTER FIVE

I couldn't help the glance I cast at Elspeth. She looked at me as well before addressing the queen again.

"Your Majesty, I never properly introduced my apprentice. This is Margaret, formerly of the House of Thoning, disowned for not wanting to marry the man of her parents' choosing."

My insides felt like they wanted to come out. I twisted my hands and endured the queen's scrutiny.

"I see. Do your parents know you're alive, child?"

I thought it humorous that she called me a child when she was barely a handful of years older than myself.

"Considering I took three dresses and a few other belongings with me when I left, I have no reason to believe they would think otherwise, Your Majesty. However, I will be sure to send them a message to let them know."

"Were there any other reports of missing children, Your Majesty?" Elspeth asked.

"None from our gentry. Many from the outlying homes near the Dark Forest."

The queen studied us both for a moment.

"I called you back here because of your frankness. And because of your willingness to sacrifice yourselves to protect the royal family. Do not think I did not notice how you continue to stand even though you suffer. Sit. Let's speak frankly."

We all sat.

"The children who are missing are not just from the outlying homes here in town. We have received word that children have been missing in towns almost a day north from here. The disappearances began the day before we received news of Turre's Queen."

"Tell me, Caster Elspeth, what do you think this means? Do you still believe this has anything to do with the magic barring the creatures from us?"

Elspeth slowly shook her head, a thoughtful frown creasing her brow.

"Have any bodies been found?" she asked after a moment.

The queen glanced down at her folded hands. Had I not witnessed her pacing moments ago, I would have thought her serene and relaxed. When she looked up, her eyes were filled with sorrow.

"One body so far. Unmarked, pale, and cold, found near a river. The parents thought the child had perhaps drowned. I'm guessing you think differently?"

"I can't say for certain, Your Majesty. But it sounds like a very perverse form of caster magic. An unnatural form of blood magic."

The queen pressed her hand to her bust and looked at a closed door.

"And will this form of caster magic be repelled indefinitely by the amulet?"

"Yes, Your Majesty."

She exhaled slowly then clapped her hands. Maids entered with refreshment. After they left, the queen asked endless questions of Elspeth about magic, and my mentor's eyes began to droop well after the tea was gone.

"Why don't you heal yourself?" the queen asked finally.

"Healing cannot be done with a temporary manipulation of energy. It's deep and altering and takes far more energy than I or any caster can channel. Those with blood magic are able to heal others; however, most will refuse as it creates an imbalance."

"That answer diminishes my faith in the trinkets you provided."

Elspeth chuckled.

"I imagine it would. Yesterday, I explained that we're all born with a different level of ability to manipulate energy, which is how some of us can perform magic. The same holds true with every plant, animal and rock that exists. However, the ability of those objects and creatures isn't in their manipulation of energy but their possession of it. That trinket is made up of four very strong items that, when combined, have the ability to not only absorb but deflect endless amounts of manipulated energy."

A knock sounded on the door from which we'd entered.

"I apologize I cannot spend more time discussing magic with you," the queen said standing.

"We understand," Elspeth said, also standing. "Your time is precious and many seek your audience."

"Your time is precious as well." The queen withdrew a leather pouch the size of my fist from her skirt pocket. "While you're here, you are not able to sell your potions. Please accept this as payment for your time."

"There is no need, Your Majesty. The coin would be better put to use helping the families who have lost lives to the woods."

"Which is why I placed extra coins in the pouch. You can go where I cannot, and I have heard that you already do so."

I accepted the purse from the queen and felt the heft of the coins inside. These were no blunt silvers or high silvers weighting the bag. She'd filled it with gold. Enough to give a coin for each missing person.

"It doesn't ease the suffering and sorrow of the families.

But perhaps it will keep food in their bellies while they grieve."

There was such true sorrow in her gaze that I knew the coin wasn't a thoughtless gift to quiet the masses but true concern from their ruler. She was doing the only thing she could.

"I hope the next time I have a need…"

"We will always answer your call," Elspeth swore, and I agreed.

THE MARKET WAS CROWDED and noisy. It felt good to sit amidst all the bustle but odd to be on the opposite side of the table. I was used to walking the streets and looking at the wares, not trying to sell my own.

Well, not my own but Elspeth's. She sat further back under the awning of her booth, trusting me to sell her potions and collect the money for each sale while she napped. Yesterday had exhausted her. She seemed in less pain today, though.

Between selling love potions that took effect just long enough for an ill-timed kiss, which led many to forced wedlock, and potions that enhanced beauty, I watched the crowds.

There were many faces that I recognized. Boys with whom I had danced and girls with whom I had spoken.

However, none of them gave me a second glance. Again, the clothes helped to disguise the face even when in plain sight.

I was only interested in one particular face, though. Atwell had promised to call on me yesterday and had never shown. I understood his concern for his father was probably foremost in his mind. However, he was foremost in mine. The night he had saved me had shown me his true character. It was a characteristic I had dared not hope to find in a boy of my own standing. My parents would be furious if I married beneath my position. But now I was free. Free from their manipulations. Free from their influence.

Not forgetting my promise to the queen, I had written a letter this morning and found a messenger as soon as I arrived at the market. By now, Mother and Father both knew I was alive and well. Elspeth was certain they would demand that I return. So I had taken precautions to ensure they would not be able to find me. I didn't want to return. Not now. Not ever. There was too much to look forward to in this life.

The day wore on, but I did not give up hope that I would see Atwell. Instead of his handsome face, I saw the familiar face of the messenger boy who lived near Elspeth's house. The one I had trusted with my letter because he never succumbed to bribery.

"I didn't expect you to return," I said when he slipped behind the booth.

He gave me a nervous look and handed me a folded and sealed bit of paper.

"I didn't say nothing," he said. "I didn't need to. They just wanted me to deliver a message back. I made sure I wasn't followed. Walked around most of the day."

I accepted the note and broke the seal as the boy ran off.

MARGARET,

Your father and I know you ran away rather than face your obligations. Since you have no love or consideration for us, we have none for you. You are dead and will remain so regardless of your letter.

Mistress of the House of Thoning

I STARED at the letter for several long moments then crumpled it into a ball.

"You shouldn't waste parchment, Margaret," Elspeth said from behind me.

"This needs to be burned."

She took the letter from me and slipped it into her pocket.

"Tonight," she promised.

I pretended not to notice her reading it when I helped the next customer.

By the time we returned to Elspeth's peaceful cottage

hours later, my feet were tired, and my lower back ached. I tried not to let my disappointment show while making our dinner. Atwell hadn't appeared at all. I hoped that he was all right and that his delay wasn't due to lack of interest but rather his need to care for his father.

"Don't let their words hurt you child," Elspeth said from her chair. I looked up from chopping carrots, a new skill I'd acquired in the last few days.

"What do you mean? Whose words?"

Elspeth chuckled and withdrew the letter from her pocket.

"If you're not thinking of this bit of nastiness, then what are you thinking of that has such a long look on your face?"

"Atwell," I said. "He was supposed to call on me yesterday. Perhaps he's so worried about his father he forgot."

"Very likely," Elspeth said. "So why don't you go remind him?"

"You mean I should go call on him?"

"Why not? You're no longer a Miss from the House of Thoning. Your parents made that quite clear. Why must you follow rules of the gentry when they no longer apply to you?"

I grinned widely. "Very true."

"Leave the carrots. I will work on dinner while you're gone. Go while it's still light. I believe Atwell Cartwright lives near the Market district. A stone and wood home that has a sign for the Cartwright's hung above the door. Ask anyone in the district, and they should be able to point you in the right direction."

I had my cloak on and was out the door before she could blink. It only took asking a few people to find out what home, and before I knew it, I stood beneath the Cartwright sign.

Taking a deep breath to settle my nerves, I straightened my skirts, squared my shoulders, and knocked on the door. The smile curling my lips was completely genuine. I tried not to think about why this boy out of all the others I'd met so deeply stirred my interest.

The door opened after the third knock. Atwell stood before me, disheveled and pale. The smile faded from my lips.

"Are you all right?"

"Yes. Margaret, I'm sorry for not calling on you as I had promised." He glanced over his shoulder, seemed to catch himself, and looked at me again. "I've been unexpectedly detained. Please don't think disfavorably of me. My intentions are still to call on you. However, I might not be able to do so for some time."

The scent of blood and wet dog tickled my nose.

As my gaze raked over Atwell again, I noted his shirt was more than just wrinkled and askew. It was stained as well. Although few, the small patches were dark. Like blood.

"Atwell, you appear to need help. Let me help you. You can trust me."

He studied me hard for a moment then opened the door wider.

"I could use assistance. I don't know..." He shook his head and motioned for me to enter.

I stepped into the darkened room, wrinkling my nose at the stronger smell. Something moved further back in the gloom, far from the banked fire.

The door shut behind me.

I squinted, trying to see what curled in the corner. The shape of a man formed. A large man.

"He returned the night before last," Atwell said. "He's badly hurt, but every time I get close to him, he tells me to get away. He says it's not safe. He's not safe."

"Your father?" I asked.

"Yes."

I stripped off my cloak and set it on the peg near the door.

"Stoke the fire so I can see better," I said.

"He doesn't like the light."

"Then we can blindfold him. But I need the light."

Atwell moved toward the fire. As the flames increased the light, Mister Cartwright's agitation increased. However, I began to see why.

Mr. Cartwright didn't look normal. His hair stuck up at all angles at different lengths. Patches appeared to be missing. Bites covered his arms, which I could see through gaps in his clothing. Atwell's father had been attacked. By what, though? I approached slowly and spoke softly.

"Mr. Cartwright? My name is Margaret. I'm here to help you."

"You cannot help me, miss."

"I would still like to try if you would allow me."

Mr. Cartwright lifted his head and turned to look at me. His eyes weren't human but rather more reminiscent of an animal. Wide pupils, and still wider irises, consumed all but the barest hint of the whites of his eyes. I swallowed my shock. In all the inferior potions and glamor spells I'd seen, none had ever gone so terribly wrong as Mr. Cartwright's.

"Will you tell me what happened?"

"Turre is in chaos. I managed a hasty trade and started home through the passage. The magic was holding; it should have been safe. But what came for me didn't come from the Dark Forest. Beasts the likes we have never seen. Claws and teeth meant to rip a man apart."

He started shaking and grunted, curling inward. The tremors jolted him so hard that his teeth clacked together repeatedly. When he settled and turned toward me, he seemed further changed, but I couldn't quite place how.

"Those they don't kill, like me, change within two days," he said bluntly. "I only returned to warn Atwell. He won't let me leave. You want to help me? Convince my son it's time to let me go."

I glanced at Atwell, who shook his head, before considering Mr. Cartwright again.

"I work with Elspeth the Caster. If you would allow me to examine you, I would like to return to her and see if there's a way we can help."

"You don't understand. I'm too far. I can feel the need to hunt, to hurt. I saw what happens to us. I wasn't the only one attacked. There are more out there. And they will want to revisit their homes and reclaim their loved ones. I won't do that to Atwell."

"I understand. Will you let me clean your wound before you go?" I extended a hand to peel back a ripped piece of jacket, and he snarled at me. I jerked back, and he closed his eyes with regret.

"No, miss. I am barely maintaining control to be the man I know I once was. The beast is rising."

I turned to Atwell. "Do you have a horse?"

He shook his head.

"I think Elspeth is our only hope. You can see something is changing him. Perhaps she can undo what's been done. But I think we need to get her quickly. She's hurt and can't walk fast."

"That won't be a problem." He reached for the door and hesitated. "Will you stay with him?"

"Of course," I said at the same time his father said, "Let me go, son. I don't want to hurt her."

Atwell pulled me close, wrapping his strong arms around me. I shivered lightly at the sensation.

"If he gets worse, run. Don't try to stop him," he whispered in my ear.

I nodded mutely and watched Atwell leave.

"It's not just the way I look that's changing," Mr. Cartright said. "My other senses are changing as well. I can smell your interest in him and his in you."

I blushed and turned toward Mr. Cartwright.

"Your son is more honorable than any man I've ever met. He saved me from some unwanted attention a week ago."

"Yes. He is honorable. That is not always a good quality."

"How so?" I asked, remaining where I was, near the door in case I needed to run.

"I came home because I didn't want him to grieve and wonder what became of me. Because he's so honorable, he is determined to keep me here to try to save me. It will cause him nothing but anguish. If I were as honorable as my son, I would leave and spare him that."

"It is your love for your son that keeps you here and that same love that gives him hope."

Mr. Cartwright nodded then made a pained noise and started shaking again. I watched the edge of his ear become less rounded and more pointed.

After a moment, he stilled.

"You said the creatures that did this to you weren't from the Dark Forest," I said softly. "Where were they from? Turre?"

"There is evil brewing there. The king is courting a new woman, and his children are missing. The people are in outrage. But I entered the dark forest passage, leaving Turre without hindrance. The beasts did not come from behind; they came up from ahead. From Drisdall."

His words created a weight in my stomach that made me ill. "How?"

"I do not know, miss." He shifted his position and cried out in pain again. When the tremors eased once more, his gruff voice put a chill in my bones.

"Open the door, miss, and go stand near the fire."

"You intend to leave before Atwell returns then?" I asked, trying to mask my fear.

"For the affection my son has for you, I intend to spare you if I lose control. The fire will keep me at bay, and the door open to the night will distract me."

I moved toward the flames and set another log on top. For good measure, I stuck the end of a long, thick branch used for stirring the coals into the flames as well.

"I cannot open the door. Not yet. For Atwell's sake, please try."

He grunted, and we continued our wait in silence. Outside, I heard the clop of hooves and a soft whinney. Mr.

Cartwright's head moved, tilting toward the sound. A low, quiet growl filled the room.

The door banged open, startling a cry from my lips. Atwell's large lean frame filled the opening. In his arms, he held Elspeth.

His concerned gaze swept over me before he focused on his father and set Elspeth down. My mentor didn't say anything as she approached Mr. Cartwright, stopping a healthy distance away.

"You were bitten?" she asked.

"Yes, several times."

"Hold out your hands and show me your teeth."

He did as she asked, and I saw claws and canines.

"The creature that bit you, what did it look like?"

"Part wolf. Part something else. Wild. An unnatural beast for sure."

"I see. I'm sorry for what you've suffered, Mr. Cartwright. And for what you will still suffer."

Atwell's father closed his eyes.

"So there is no hope?" Atwell asked, his voice flat.

I went to him and took his hand in mine. Elspeth moved toward us.

"Your father isn't changing because of a simple potion gone wrong. He's turning into something I have little knowledge of. What I know is that no one survives a bite unchanged for life. While I cannot help your father, there is hope for you," Elspeth said. "For all of us if your father can tell us more."

Mr. Cartwright repeated everything he'd told me. While he spoke, Atwell's thumb smoothed over the back of my hand again and again. I didn't think he knew what he did. Rather, he was hurting and seeking comfort from me without intent.

"Let us be done," Mr. Cartwright said. "Leave this house so I may speak with my son."

Elspeth reached into her cloak and withdrew a sharp knife which she handed to Atwell.

"The man that was your father is almost gone. Do not take long to say farewell."

Elspeth grabbed me by the elbow and dragged me outside with more force than I thought her capable.

"Hurry girl. We need to get to the smith."

"What about Atwell?"

"They will either kill each other, or they won't."

She hurried away on foot, ignoring the horse.

"Is that why you left Atwell the knife?" I asked, hurrying after her. "You think he'll kill his father."

"I know he won't. I left the knife so he can defend himself when his father loses himself. Now stop talking and move. We have much to do before morning."

We'd only made it around the corner when a horse's scream, and a beast's triumphant howl, tore through the air.

CHAPTER SIX

TERROR GRIPPED ME DURING OUR RACE TO THE CASTLE. Hearing the horse cry out and the beast's howl had struck fear in my heart. That Elspeth had stolen one of the smith's horses had made my blood run cold.

With my arms wrapped around Elspeth's waist, I hung on tightly, listening to the clatter of the horse's hooves on the cobble. Prior to this night, I would have sworn she would never steal or press the animal as hard as she was. That she had could only mean terrible things.

Elspeth suddenly pulled back on the reins. She was off the horse, me toppling gracelessly with her, the moment the steed stopped.

"Take me to the queen."

Disoriented and trying to right my skirts, I looked up to see we'd arrived at the gate. Elspeth marched toward the posted guards even as they raised their spears at her.

"Stick me with one of those, and your cocks will wither to useless brown stumps before the sun rises. Open the damn gate. Now. Or I shall do it for you."

The guards must have seen something in Elspeth's eyes to back her threat, for they lowered their weapons and opened the gate.

"Come, Margaret. Lift those skirts and show some leg. We have very little time."

The guard and I shared a shocked look as she lifted her skirts and took off running. I hurried to do the same, trying my best to keep up with Elspeth while the guard did his best to keep up with me.

The set of guards at the next gate saw us coming and were smart enough to open the door. One of them ran ahead.

Winded by the time we reached the top of the steps, I was grateful for the small pause as the guard knocked on the queen's door.

This time a real maid answered, poking her head through a small gap to peer at us.

"Her Majesty sleeps," she whispered.

Elspeth slapped her hand against the panel.

"Wake the queen, or we all die."

"Open the door, Jane," a familiar voice called. The maid quickly admitted us.

The queen was already sitting up in her large bed. Her

hair was pulled back in a single braid hanging over one shoulder of her modest dressing down.

"Elspeth. Margaret. Why are you here?" As she asked, she drew back the covers and got out of bed.

"Your kingdom is under attack. Creatures that spread disease through bites or scratches have come through from the Dark Forest."

"How many?" the queen demanded, tightening her robe.

"By now, every missing person is one. Double that number to account for the creatures that turn them. And double that number again to account for how many will be taken this night."

"How do we stop them?"

"They came from the passage and hide in the forest in the light of day. The pillars must be destroyed."

The queen stared at Elspeth. I looked at my friend, too. Much like the amulets we'd created, the pillars were the stone sentinels that created the passage between the two kingdoms, an enchanted tunnel of safety that the creatures of the wood could not enter. Without them, travel would not be possible to Turre, or from Turre to Drisdall.

"The pillars?"

"There is no other way."

"Turre will see it as an act of aggression."

"A reliable witness says Turre is in a state of turmoil.

Likely they are suffering as we are. I believe destroying the pillars will no longer matter to our neighboring kingdom."

"Very well. It will be done."

Elspeth started to turn away without her usual bow then paused, seeming to remember herself, and gave a quick incline of her head before rushing out the door.

The queen glanced at me in question as I also moved toward her door.

"The creatures fear the light," I said in a rush. "Anyone bitten tonight will not fully change for two days."

I caught up with Elspeth on the stairs.

"Where are we going?" I whispered.

"To the Brazen Belle to protect those we can until dawn's first light."

Elspeth's sense of urgency felt misplaced in the quiet darkness outside the castle. Nothing howled. Nothing stirred. I did not try to convince myself that she was wrong, however. I had seen Mr. Cartwright. I had heard his story. I knew danger was out there.

The race back through town ended abruptly at the cottage.

"I thought we were going to the Brazen Belle," I said when she slid off the horse's back.

"I am going to the Brazen Belle. You are staying here."

She pushed her door open and immediately went to the potions she had stored on the shelves. She pulled three vials from their number and handed them to me.

As soon as they were in my hands, she gripped my face firmly.

"Can I trust you, child?"

"Of course."

"Then listen closely."

"You will mix these three vials together. You will put five drops in as many new vials as the mixture will fill. If someone comes to this door asking for help for a bite, you will give them a vial. No matter who it is, you will give them a vial even if it be the king."

I looked in Elspeth's eyes and saw the fear there.

"The drops will kill them?" I asked.

"It is the only way to stop this from spreading. Say nothing. Give them the vial and watch them drink it and send them on their way. Do you understand?"

"I understand." Too well. This would ruin Elspeth. No one would trust her after this night.

"Stay in this house. These walls will protect you."

She left in a flurry of skirts and cloak, and I heard the horse's hooves a moment later.

I fixed the potions, stoked the fire, and lit the candles so everyone would know someone was awake here. Despite the hour, I wasn't tired. I paced and watched the door. It wasn't long before the first knock broke the silence.

Gripping a vial in my palm, I opened the door and froze. Atwell stood in the opening. My gaze swept over him, looking for signs of injury, while my heart beat wildly.

"Are you hurt? Did your father bite you?"

"No. I'm not injured. He spoke to me, ordered me to stay inside this night, then ran out the door."

"Come in."

He entered and faced me as I closed the door against what might still prowl the darkness.

"Why did you leave your house if your father warned you to stay inside?"

"I waited until I knew he left. I had to see you. I needed to be sure you made it safely home. That Elspeth will keep you safe." He tore his gaze from mine and looked around the room. "Where is Elspeth?"

"She is trying to keep the people of Drisdall safe. She left me here to care for any bitten who ask for help." I showed him the vial in my palm. "She told the queen it has to be stopped."

He looked down at the vial.

"The families will come for her afterward. They'll come for you."

I swallowed hard and nodded.

"I know. But, I also know we don't have a choice. You should have seen Elspeth's fear. I think if we don't stop this, our futures will be even worse."

He reached for me and slowly pulled me into his arms. I rested my head on his shoulder and absorbed what comfort he offered.

"Then we all need to do what we must to ensure our futures," he said softly.

Our embrace was far from appropriate, but after what we'd both endured this night, I couldn't withdraw. I didn't want to. Instead, I relished the way his breath tickled the side of my head and the feel of his hands pressed against my back.

"I must go," he said softly. "My father left some business unfinished that needs to be addressed immediately."

I lifted my head and found the position placed our mouths far too close. My gaze flicked to his lips then up again.

"Don't leave."

He reached up and gently ran the backs of his fingers along my cheek.

"You have no idea how you tempt me to stay." This time it was his gaze that dropped to my mouth. My pulse quickened, and his head dipped ever so slightly. I held my breath waiting for the first touch of his lips to mine.

Instead, he drew back.

"Forgive me, Margaret. The night has robbed me of my decency."

"I've never met a man more decent, Atwell. There's nothing to forgive." I stood on my toes and pressed my lips to his. His hold on me tightened as his mouth brushed against mine.

When I pulled back, my cheeks were flushed.

"Given your father's fear of the fire light, it would be safer to wait until morning to avoid any other creatures lurking in the dark."

Atwell studied me for a moment.

"I fear I cannot wait."

I could see the regret and determination in his gaze. Whatever business pulled at him, it did so with an insistency I had no hope of matching.

"Then let me give you something to keep you safe." I dug through Elspeth's chest of magical items, hoping I wasn't making a foolish mistake. The small wooden cylinder attached to a leather cord lay near the bottom, wrapped in a fine cloth.

"Here," I said, handing it to him. "Wear this around your neck."

"What is it?"

"I don't know. I only know that when you open the cylinder, there is a crystal that shines so brightly it will blind you even with your eyes closed. Use it only if there is no other choice."

He reached for my other hand and gently uncurled my fingers from around the small vial I still held.

"And this," he said. "In case there is no other choice. I don't want to come back and hurt those I might love."

My throat grew tight looking at him, and I nodded. He took the vial, brushed a kiss on my forehead, and left.

Atwell's vial wasn't the last I gave out that night. With a

breaking heart, I watched the sunrise and looked at the three vials remaining. Elspeth returned not long after to find me sitting by the fire, quiet tears running down my cheeks.

"How many?" she asked.

"Twenty-three," I said. "Three remain."

"Come. Help me make some more. We'll need to give them out at the market too before the call goes out."

I looked up at Elspeth and saw the dark circles under her eyes.

"Is there no other way but death?"

"Theirs or ours?"

"Both."

"If there is, I do not know it. And neither do those who I've asked." She came to me and set a hand on my head. "I would spare everyone if I could."

"Atwell came last night. He took a vial in case he's bitten while addressing some business his father left unfinished."

Elspeth's gaze filled with pity.

"He means much to you."

"More than he probably should."

She tugged me to my feet and hugged me. The embrace comforted some of the ache and dried my tears.

Together we made the potion. When I admitted I'd given the stone, Elspeth hadn't been angry, only worried for Atwell, stating the power of the crystal was unpredictable.

"You were right to give it to him. The light might have

saved him last night. We will collect it from him after the market."

It didn't take us long to make a new batch of vials. However, our steps were slow on the way to the market. I wasn't sure if it was a night without sleep or the thought of handing out more vials that delayed us. Yet, even despite the late hour, the market wasn't its usual hub of activity. While the number of people clogging the way seemed the same, the mood was far more subdued.

"Did you hear the baker's son is missing?" the man who owned the stall next to Elspeth asked. "Disappeared overnight. He's not the only one. Some disappear, and some don't."

"Some don't?" I asked, prompting him to continue.

"A girl not far from my home was bitten after something jumped through her window. It was big enough to break away the stone holding the shutter. The bite was so deep, she didn't live the night."

He shook his head slowly. "I didn't hear a thing."

As Elspeth predicted, the booth was busy. People seemed to know that the bites were unnatural and to be feared. Those who stopped at the booth were quiet and secretive about their requests for help.

"My neighbor came to you with his wife last night," one woman said after stating her husband was bitten on the arm. "I heard she died this morning."

"I've never been a healer," Elspeth said. "And I know

my apprentice didn't promise such a thing." Elspeth offered the woman a vial. "This isn't a cure. There is no cure. No one will heal from these bites. This is to help ease the suffering."

I watched the sorrow, anger, then fear cloud her features before everything cleared. Woodenly, she accepted the vial.

"We've three children," she said softly.

"You're protecting them from the same fate," Elspeth said.

I hurt for the woman and what she needed to do to keep her children safe. In that moment, I knew I too would do anything to keep any child I had safe from harm. I wouldn't be my parents. Indifferent and self-serving just to follow social norms. No, I would love any child I had and enjoy watching them grow. I would protect them with my last breath, and I hoped my future husband would do the same. The image of Atwell rose to my mind, and I forced myself to focus on the present.

Across the way, I watched a lean man struggle under the weight of several parcels. Even as he struggled, he stopped at a stall to purchase grain and carrots.

"I'm going to help him," I said to Elspeth, already rushing off. I needed to do something selflessly helpful. Something that didn't result in someone's death.

"Can I carry that for you, sir?" I asked just as the vendor was about to hand the new parcel over. "It looks like your hands are already full."

A man with brown hair peeked around the packages.

"Thank you, miss. Your help is much welcome."

I accepted the parcel for him and followed him along the way where he stopped twice more.

"I normally don't make purchases like this," he said. "I'm taking my wife north." He lowered his voice. "It's not safe here."

No sooner had he said that than a child ran by shouting, "The king's men are trying to bring down the pillars!" He repeated the message as he continued on his way.

"It will be safer once the pillars are down," I said to the man.

"I'm not so certain. So many have already fallen ill." We turned onto a street where I followed him to a wagon in which a woman, not much older than me, sat waiting with two young children.

"Allow me to introduce my wife, Nadelle," the man said, "and my daughter's Bryn and Blye."

"Hello. My name's Margaret."

Nadelle smiled at me but did not get down from her perch on the seat to help us with the packages. She didn't look well. Pale.

"Was she bitten?" I asked the man softly.

He jerked his head up from fitting his supplies in the back of the wagon and looked at me in surprise.

"Not at all. She's with child. The babe is still new and letting her know it's there through bouts of sickness."

"Oh. I apologize."

"Don't," Nadelle said with a weak smile. "Given the state of affairs here, I think it right that you ask. Bernard, darling, can you bring the water flask up front when you're finished?"

"Are you sure that will settle well in your stomach just before we travel?"

"Of course not. However, rinsing my mouth after little Bernard is done making his presence known will help us be on our way sooner."

Bernard gave me a sheepish smile before grabbing the flask.

"Thank you again for your help, Margaret."

"Good luck on your journey north, sir."

He offered his hand. "Bernard Hovtell, teacher. No need for sir."

I waved them off and returned to Elspeth's stall.

"Did you hear the boy before?" I asked her.

"Yes. The pillars," she said, looking at me with concern. "They are close to bringing them down. Anything unnatural within the Dark Forest will no longer be able to attack Drisdall."

"That's good news, Elspeth. We'll only need to worry about those bitten then."

My mentor continued to look worried.

"Is that not true?" I asked.

"It is. With the passage closed, we are much safer."

"Why the concern, then?"

"I also heard something else. A certain young man went into the Dark Forest well before dawn in search of his father's abandoned wagon."

It took a moment for me to understand what she was saying.

"Atwell? That was the business to which he needed to attend?" My gaze shifted to the rooftops to the west, the direction of the forest. "How long does he have until the pillars fall?"

"The pillars will not prevent his return," she said, continuing to watch me expectantly.

"But everything that's trapped in there with him will," I said, understanding the crux of the situation. Atwell had entered the passage when the creatures were in town. With dawn, the creatures had returned. With the fall of the pillars, the barrier that created the passage would fall, and all the creatures of the forest would be able to reach him.

My heart fractured with a pain so intense it numbed me.

"Why is life so cruel?" I asked. "Why did I meet him at all?"

Elspeth hugged me for a moment.

"Many ask that very question every day. The pain is part of life, imp. It's as natural as our ability to heal from it."

The way she spoke...it was as if he were already dead.

"Come, it's time we return to the cottage. We both need sleep before the sun sets."

I wiped my face and looked out over the Market. The crowds were thinning, likely due to hunger for a midday meal.

The walk back to the cottage was quiet. Elspeth made us a simple soup, and we ate in silence. I felt the ground rumble through the soles of my feet. It lasted only a moment. Not long after, I heard the calls in the streets that the pillars had fallen.

"I'm going to go lie down," I said.

It barely felt like I'd slept when pounding on the door woke me.

"By the order of King Aftan, open this door."

I sat up in bed, scarcely noting the dim light as I struggled to understand what was happening.

"Hush," Elspeth said, looking at me when I leaned forward to see over the edge of the loft. She waved me back as she reached for the door.

I lay back down, listening over the nervous hammer of my heart.

"Are you Elspeth the Caster?" a man asked.

"I am."

"The king summons you."

"Very well. I need my cloak."

"Where is the other caster?"

My heart started to race. I had no doubt he meant me. Why were we being summoned?

"There is no caster, sir."

"An apprentice, then. Where is she?"

I could feel Elspeth's defeat in the moment of silence that followed.

"Margaret, wake up. We must see the king."

CHAPTER SEVEN

WE WALKED BETWEEN TWO SETS OF GUARDS. THERE were no horses, but I didn't mind. The night was too quiet for the noise their hooves would make. Instead, we walked by the light of candles mounted inside metal lanterns.

We'd barely made any progress toward the castle when a growl came from the dark between two homes.

"Do not leave the circle of light," Elspeth warned.

The fore guards readied their spears while those behind us readied their bows.

"I see it," one of the men behind us whispered a moment before an arrow flew past my head. The solid thump echoed as another arrow let loose. The beast howled then fell with a thud. The men with the lanterns moved forward.

Elspeth grabbed my hand to keep me in place. Despite

my reservations about standing in the shadows, I stayed at her side while they shone the light on the fallen beast. Ears, shaped like a wolf's, protruded from the sides of its head. Its snout was thicker like that of a bear. Fur covered its head.

It was part wolf and part bear as Mr. Cartwright said. However, it did not have an animal's legs. It had the arms and legs of a man.

"Why is it wearing pants?" one of the guards asked softly.

"Because it was once a man."

He glanced at Elspeth then motioned for his men to group around us again. Although that was our only delay in reaching the castle, it wasn't the only disturbance. Twice more, a howl broke out in the night.

"Too many remained," Elspeth said quietly. Whether to herself or me, I couldn't be sure.

Instead of taking us around to the side gate, we approached the castle from the front. White pillars gleamed in the light of the long pole lanterns lining the approach. This time, I did see the people in their pretty clothes. They lined the lawns and stairs, speaking in quiet tones in small groups while casting angry glances our way as we passed. Inside the towering doors was much of the same. Our heels echoed on the polished stone floors, and I idly wondered what magic had been used to create such splendor, for the work-worn hands of man alone could not have accomplished such a feat.

I felt no thrill as we approached the open doors to the main court. I felt very little of anything but the pain of knowing that Atwell was likely dead.

People stood off to the sides, speaking in low tones as Elspeth and I walked down the center of the vast space toward the occupied thrones at the other end. Twin crowns adorned the heads of the man and woman there, letting me know precisely who they were as if the room and grandeur weren't enough.

The queen looked like a queen, dressed in a gown appropriately ruffled and embroidered. The man beside her, the king of Drisdall, was younger than I'd pictured him. With brown hair yet untouched by white, he looked stern and watched us with an angry light in his eyes.

As soon as we stopped before the king and queen, a hush fell over the room.

"You are charged with the deaths of over two dozen of Drisdall's people," the king said, looking at Elspeth. "What do you say to these charges?"

"That I am guilty," I said, stepping forward.

"Your Majesties, she knows not of which she speaks," Elspeth said quickly. "Her heart is broken over the loss of her sweetheart. He went into the passages last evening and did not return before the pillars were destroyed."

I understood very well of what I spoke just as I understood that the king and queen were looking to pacify their "good" people who were outraged. There was only one penalty for murder, and I'd already lost one person whom I cared about. I would not lose another.

"My grief does not change the fact I mixed together the potion and handed out the vials to those who were bitten."

The queen sat forward slightly.

"Bitten?"

Elspeth, who'd stepped forward to stand beside me, pinched my arm in warning.

"Bitten by the beasts that came from the passage. Those bitten were doomed to become beasts as well."

The king leaned forward.

"What proof do you have that such speculations would come to be? What proof do you have that any bitten person could not be healed?"

"Your guards killed a beast tonight. A creature with pointed ears, a muzzle filled with teeth, and a body covered with fur. Yet, the shape of its limbs resembled man more than wolf or bear, and it still wore pants. I have no proof that it cannot be cured, only proof of how quickly the sickness spreads. Anyone bitten will change within two nights. And those changed will bite more."

The king called for the guards.

"What did you see?" he demanded.

"It is as she says. It was a beast who appeared to have once been a man."

Murmurs broke out over the court, and the king called for silence.

"What was in the vials?" the queen asked.

"A simple herbal mixture to dull any pain and weaken the body, allowing the person to find peace before the corruption can take hold," Elspeth said.

"And if your apprentice's sweetheart returned bitten, would you administer a vial to him?"

"She wouldn't need to, Your Majesty," I said, my insides dying even more. "He understood what was happening and took a vial with him should he be bitten."

"And you believe he would drink it? That he would bring about his own death?"

"To spare those he loves from turning into the same, he would."

"And that is what these creatures do. They return to their family. To their friends," Elspeth added. Gasps rang out behind us. "If left unchecked, there will be no people of Drisdall. Every man, woman, and child will become a beast."

Murmurs rose in the room, creating a din. The king did nothing to quiet them. Instead, he studied Elspeth and me. After a few moments, he lifted a hand, which silenced everyone.

"Are you saying that you murdered people for the safety of the kingdom?" the king asked Elspeth.

"I am saying that I did no more than the guards who escorted us here tonight."

The king sat back in his throne, his expression giving nothing away.

"Clear the room."

Elspeth took my hand, and together we waited for everyone to leave except the guards stationed by the king and queen. When the doors closed with finality, the king stood, and the guards flanked him, hands on their swords.

If Elspeth died with me, would there be anyone left to notice my absence?

The king looked at his guard.

"I expect it will not take long for word to spread. Make it known that all bitten who come forth will receive ten gold coins which the crown will gift to whomever the bitten names."

The guard nodded and strode toward a side door.

"You have done a service to the kingdom at a great risk to yourself. Yet, I cannot let these killings, which were unsanctioned by the king, go unaddressed."

The king looked at both of us as if expecting a response.

"Then, sanction them," the queen said, standing. "As you said, these women have done the kingdom a service."

The king continued to watch us as the queen approached and bowed her head to Elspeth then to me.

"Did you really give your young man a vial?" she asked me.

"Yes, Your Majesty." Though I hadn't. He'd taken it. Atwell was a better man than any I would ever know.

"Aftan, see her pain. The caster and her apprentice didn't wish to harm anyone. It was their wish to keep people safe that prompted the need for immediate action." She turned to the king and his inclined his head.

"It will be done," he said.

"What will be done with those to come forward?" she asked.

"They will be given a choice. Walk into the Dark Forest while they still can, or take the caster's potion."

Elspeth's fingers twitched on my hand.

"We have few vials, Your Majesty," she said. "I can make some more, but it will take time."

"We will hold those who choose death until you return. Go."

He turned his back to us, and the queen gave a small smile before she dipped her head and followed her husband to the thrones.

Without Elspeth's hold, I might have stood in the throne room forever. The cool air cleared my head when we reached the steps leading down to the lawns, which were full of people. The same four guards fell into place around us as we descended.

Fear had replaced the angry glares from earlier. The people of Drisdall no longer condemned us. They feared what was to come.

"REST WHILE I STRAIN THE TINCTURES," Elspeth said.

Behind her, the sky was starting to lighten. While exhausted, I wasn't ready to sleep. Grinding the herbs then shaking the black flasks for hours had kept me busy. However, idle hands now allowed my thoughts to roam.

They returned to Atwell. I couldn't stop imagining what might have become of him. Was he now running with the beasts in the Dark Forest? Was he perhaps the beast the guards killed? No. It hadn't been long enough for either situation. Was he dead amongst the trees with no one to mourn his passing?

"Can we scry for Atwell?" I asked Elspeth. "Like we did for his father?"

She stopped what she was doing to look at me.

"What do you hope to see?"

"Nothing. It will give me peace that he's not lost in the forest forever, suffering an existence he did not want."

"And if he is?"

I sighed and looked out the window.

"I'll find a way to live with that knowledge."

She came and sat beside me.

"He means so much to you?"

"It's odd, isn't it? We barely know one another. Yet, from the moment I met him, he has occupied the recesses of my mind. I cannot seem to let the thought of him go."

Elspeth nodded slowly.

"Love comes in many forms. Some are so large they cannot be contained. That kind of love is easy to see and recognize. Some are smaller, subtler. It makes the love no less meaningful, only harder to see for what it is."

I thought about Atwell and what I felt for him. The concern. The desire to see him again. The way it felt when he held me.

"I do care for Atwell. But love?"

Elspeth gave me a small smile. "We shall see."

She stood and started preparing everything, leaving the poison to rest. When she started speaking the words, I stood and went to her side.

The water shimmered in the bowl as it had before, the mist rising in two places. Turre still remained a murky outline while Drisdall cleared. No small speck of green moved within the boundaries of the Dark Forest. It moved within Drisdall.

"What does it mean that he's here?" I asked, jerking my gaze up, daring to hope.

Elspeth clasped my arms firmly.

"One of two things. He's returned to you unharmed. Or he lost his vial and will ask for another."

My chest ached with anticipation and fear.

Elspeth pressed one of the remaining vials in my hand.

"Go. Find Atwell before the guards do."

I raced from the cottage, not bothering with a cloak. The

thump of my feet hitting dirt echoed in the early morning light. No one stirred at this hour, so I ran unhindered until I reached the Market district. There, guards patrolled. I had to answer why I was out so early before they would let me pass.

Atwell answered his door after my third knock. I barely had time to focus on his tired face before he pulled me into his arms. I held him tightly, shaking.

"Tell me you're all right. Tell me you're not bitten."

"I'm unbitten, Margaret, because of you. And because of my father."

He loosened his hold on me just enough to lead me inside and close the door.

"What do you mean, your father?"

Atwell led me to a chair. While I sat, he paced before the fire.

"The passage was clear when I first entered it. Not long after, I heard the creatures enter. I had a torch for the darker tracks of the passage and the horses. Between the two, I kept out of the beasts' reaches. Just after midday, I found the wagon my father was forced to abandon. It sat in a spot of sunlight. As soon as I moved to hitch the horses to it, they flooded the surrounding shadows. I went to the horses and covered their eyes then my own. Even covered, I could see the light when I uncapped the crystal. The beasts screamed and ran. I quickly fled with the wagon as well. It wasn't long before they were behind me, racing to catch me.

"Another creature came from the darkened trees within the passage. He fought back any who grew too close. At first, I thought he was staking his claim. Then, I felt the pillars fall. The horses spooked and veered too close to a tree, clipping the wagon and almost knocking it over. The beast hit it from the other side to right us and said one word.

"Run."

Atwell stopped his pacing and looked at me.

"After that, the creature took off into the trees like the rest of them." Atwell sighed and looked around the room. "He looked nothing like my father. I might be wrong. But it helps thinking it was him."

I nodded, understanding what he meant.

"During that time, I lost the crystal. Thankfully, I didn't need it again."

"The crystal means nothing. I'm only grateful you returned." We studied each other for a long moment. "How long ago did you return?" I asked. "You look tired."

"I am. I haven't slept in days. Since my father first returned."

I stood.

"I should leave you to rest."

He caught my arm and stopped me from doing as I said.

"Please stay."

The desperate look in his eyes drew me in. He slowly pulled me to his chest. This time, when his lips met mine, it was no chaste meeting of skin. His tongue swept over my bottom lip, coaxing me to open as his arms wrapped around me. I couldn't resist him.

Granting him entrance, he stole my breath with the first stroke of his tongue against mine. His hands delved into my hair, and he kissed me with an intensity that stole my awareness of the world outside his home. There were only his hands, his mouth, and a growing need I'd never felt before.

I tore my lips from him and stared up at his handsome face. His gaze held mine, his breathing erratic.

"I've never met anyone like you," I said. "Since the moment you stepped out of the shadows, you've occupied my thoughts."

His fingers brushed over my jaw then traced my lips. A warmth spread through me at his focused attention to every detail.

"I've never met anyone like you, either, Margaret. You steal my breath and rob me of thought. You fill my mind day and night."

I swallowed hard as he closed the distance and kissed me again. I lifted my hands and set them on his strong shoulders. Nothing before had ever felt so right as me in Atwell's arms, kissing him as if I had found my reason for living. And I believed I had.

When he next lifted his head so we could catch our breaths, I slipped from his arms. I was tired of rules and others trying to decide what my life should be. I wanted to take control. To be the one to decide. I wanted Atwell.

Taking a steadying breath, I slipped out of my dress and stood before him in my underthings. His hungry gaze swept over me. Slowly, he reached out and gave the cords at my waist and throat light tugs. That was all it took for the remaining material covering me fell to the floor.

"Margaret," he said. The hoarse need in his voice created an ache between my legs.

He fell to his knees before me and kissed the skin just below my navel. A shiver stole through me and ignited a fire within my belly. I threaded my fingers in his hair, needing him to kiss me there again. His breath teased me as he trailed more kisses lower. Then he stilled.

"I cannot take what you offer until you answer a question that's been in my mind since the moment you bashed the man with the piss pot."

I giggled and ran my finger along the curve of his cheekbone.

"What question?" I asked.

"Will you marry me, Margaret? Will you be mine forever?"

"Yes."

He stood and picked me up, carrying me to a small room off the main living area. There, he set me on the bed. His eyes never left me as he disrobed. I struggled not to blush as

I looked at him. His arms were thick and full of muscled ridges, like his chest, stomach, and...

I swallowed hard at the jutting piece of him that would join with me. I knew how it was done. I'd seen my father's horses mating and had asked Elspeth about it.

"You look worried," he said. "Have you changed your mind?"

I shook my head and beckoned him to lay beside me. He smiled as he joined me and trailed his fingers over my skin. The feel of him banished thoughts of what was to come as I lost myself to the sensations of the moment. The way he explored the ridge of my hip, the dip of my stomach, and the valley between my breasts. His lips met mine as his hand covered one mound. A small sound escaped me at the heat of him. His mouth left mine. Panting for air, I struggled to exist beyond the trailing kisses he made from my jaw, down my throat, to my nipple. I cried out when his mouth closed over the peak and suckled. The feel of his fingers on my leg didn't register until he nudged them apart.

He caressed my folds, driving the need growing within me to the point of desperation. Then he touched me in a way that shattered everything. I arched off the bed, my cry of joy lost to his lips. Before the pleasure could recede, his weight settled on me. I felt the heat of his cock against my pulsing core and lifted my hips as I kissed him feverishly.

The stab of pain cooled the heat and robbed me of the lingering pleasure.

"I'm sorry," he whispered in my ear. "Hold still for just a moment."

As I held still, he kissed a trail along my jaw, and his fingers found my nipple. Like a cord connected the two, each time his fingers plucked the sensitive bud, a spasm of pleasure rippled between my legs where he was seated.

Atwell groaned and shifted forward ever so slightly. The sensation made me gasp and arch into him. He nipped my nipple and withdrew only to return again. The heat returned with each thrust and soon I found myself panting and reaching for the joy I'd known before he'd entered me.

He jerked within me, the rhythm stuttering for a moment before intensifying. The heat, his strong thrusts, and feel of him inside of me shattered me again. With a cry, I embraced the joy.

In a sweaty heap, we lay together, our breathing calming.

"We'll have a life together, Margaret. And I will do everything within my power to make sure you love every day of it."

I kissed him lightly and closed my eyes. I was already loving it.

THE MARKET WAS alive with noise when we emerged several hours later after Atwell had slept.

"Are you sure you wouldn't rather sleep some more?" I asked. I needed to return to Elspeth. Not only did I need to help deliver the vials to the palace, I needed to tell her about Atwell. And he'd insisted on joining me.

His fingers threaded through mine.

"I wouldn't be able to leave your side if I tried."

I smiled and walked with him to the cottage. We spoke of so many things along the way. His trading plans for the lemons and other goods that had been in the wagon. My plans for the house we would now share. Our hopes for the future. The children we would have. How much we both would enjoy making the children.

A blush colored my cheeks when we reached Elspeth's. She took one look at me and smiled knowingly.

"It appears all is well," she said.

"It is," I said. I smiled as Atwell looked down at me with complete adoration in his eyes before facing Elspeth.

"Margaret explained what happened with her parents. No woman should wed without family at her side. Will you stand in their place? Will you grant me permission to wed Margaret in their stead?"

"Yes." She hugged me tightly then briskly ordered us to help her deliver vials to the palace.

We didn't go through the side gate but through the main entrance. The guards didn't question us. And there were far fewer people present. Instead of the throne room, we met with someone in another room and explained how the vials worked. Atwell was tasked with helping the man distribute the vials to those in the dungeon while Elspeth and I were escorted to the queen.

CHAPTER EIGHT

THE QUEEN STOPPED HER PACING THE MOMENT WE entered.

"Your Majesty," Elspeth said with a curtsy. I quickly did the same.

"Elspeth, you've helped my family and my people beyond measure. At great risk to yourself. You've won my trust. I pray it's not misplaced."

"Never, Your Majesty."

"I have another request of you. Since the birth of Prince Greydon, my husband has wanted another heir to ensure the throne. I seek your advice. Do you have knowledge of anything that might help?"

"There are teas that can help. Are your menstruations regular?"

"They are. And I've been drinking teas, but they haven't worked."

"These things take time. Please excuse my boldness, but how often do you lay with your husband?"

The queen looked aside.

"I find the task trying and don't often open my bed to him."

She glanced up in time to catch the surprise on my face.

"You will learn soon enough that the task isn't always agreeable. I heard that your man returned from the forest unharmed."

"Yes, Your Majesty. This morning."

"I am happy for his safe return." She looked at Elspeth. "Should we discuss this without your apprentice?"

Elspeth laughed.

"She plans to wed soon. It is better she gains what knowledge she can before then." She gestured the queen to a chair. "I will prepare some new teas for you to drink daily. Along with that, might I suggest a bath immediately before inviting the king to bed you? It will relax you and might make the experience more enjoyable. I also recommend opening your bed to him at least every third day."

The queen nodded, a hint of resignation in her eyes. I hoped I would never look like that at the thought of bedding Atwell. My skin tingled at the memory of our recent bedding, and I knew he would always be welcomed by me.

"WELL, KISS HER ALREADY, BOY," Elspeth said.

She chuckled when Atwell's lips met mine in a brief, chaste kiss.

"I will see you before dusk," he said.

I nodded and watched him walk away. My heart couldn't have been fuller. And although I craved to bask in my husband's adoration, I knew there would be time enough for that later.

In many ways, not much had changed over the past month. I continued to assist as Elspeth's apprentice, and Elspeth and I still visited the queen often. The number of people reported missing had diminished with each passing day. As had the beast sightings at night. The last one had been killed over a week ago.

In other ways, everything had changed. I lived with Atwell as the new Mrs. Cartwright, secret friend of the queen of Drisdall. I'd found a purpose and place in life and loved every moment of it.

The queen greeted us with tea and cakes in her private chambers.

"You look pleased," I said, noting the color in her cheeks.

"Very pleased. The warm baths and time have improved my outlook on nightly visits. The king's attentions are," the color in her cheeks darkened, "most welcome."

"I'm happy for you, Your Majesty," Elspeth said. My

encouraging and Elspeth's herbal knowledge had done much to help the queen overcome her distaste of bed play.

"And," the queen added, "although it is too soon to make any announcement, I missed my cycle."

"Congratulations, Your Majesty," Elspeth said then glanced at me.

"When was your last cycle, Margaret?"

Still smiling from the queen's news, I looked at my friend in confusion.

"Cycle?" I thought back. And realized I hadn't had one since I'd left home. My smile faded then reappeared twice as big.

"It seems that congratulations are due to both of you ladies," Elspeth said.

A door burst open.

"It's getting worse, Sevil. Ten were found by—"

The king stopped short at the sight of us. Elspeth stood and curtsied. I did the same.

"Excuse us," he said abruptly.

We turned to leave, but the queen stopped us.

"Elspeth. Margaret. Wait. Aftan, I know how you feel about magic, but I'm begging you to entrust them with your confidence. They helped us once. Perhaps they can—"

A bright blue light emanated from the neckline of the queen's gown. A twin light came from under the king's neckcloth.

The king and queen both gasped. The king reached for

his amulet, and Sevil launched herself at him to smack his hand away.

"Do not!"

A little boy came running into the room.

"Mother! The necklace is glowing. I didn't touch it like you said."

"You're a very good boy, Greydon," she said, still holding her husband's gaze. "It needs to stay in contact with your skin to protect you." King Aftan lowered his hand.

"How long will this glow?" he asked, directing the question at Elspeth.

"The duration of the spell directed at you."

No sooner had she said the words than the glow faded. The royal family remained whole and healthy. A cry went up somewhere within the castle. It wasn't long after that someone entered at a run.

"Your Majesty. The royal advisers are dead."

"All of them?"

"All twelve."

The king glanced at us and dismissed the messenger with a wave of his hand.

"Greydon, find your teacher, and tell him you will be joining us for dinner."

Once the boy was gone and the door closed, the king faced Elspeth.

"There are no more bitten. The last one was put to death five days after the pillars fell."

"The missing people?" she asked.

"They are not missing. Each one was discovered, dead."

"How long after they were reported missing?"

"A day or two at most."

"What do you think it is?" the queen asked.

"The use of a corrupt form of blood magic in an attempt to rid Drisdall of its rulers."

The king swore and started pacing. The queen's hand went to the flat of her stomach.

"What about the babe?" she asked.

The king stopped pacing to look at the queen.

"Babe?"

She smiled slightly and nodded.

"Why didn't you tell me?"

"I didn't want you to stop—" She blushed.

"Never."

"I don't believe the babe was harmed," Elspeth said before the moment grew too uncomfortable. "The magic was directed at you and deflected by the charm. However, if it becomes known that you are with child, the magic could be directed at the babe. There is no protection of which I know."

"Whoever is doing this must be stopped," the king vowed. He kissed his wife's temple and left her chambers.

By the time we left the castle, there were already handwritten decrees on all the public announcement boards.

. . .

ALL MAGIC IS FORBIDDEN in the kingdom of Drisdall, and any person found practicing it will be sent to the Dark Forest. Those with knowledge of those practicing it should report to the head guard.

"I HOPE we don't see the inside of a dungeon cell because of this," I said.

"IT FEELS like I've eaten half a nest of rabbits," I said as I lay wrapped in Atwell's arms. His fingers trailed over the swell of my stomach.

"It looks like you have several nests of rabbits in there."

I swatted his hand.

"I should have never told you that I carry two babes."

"Why? You would prefer that I think you an overly large woman?"

"Atwell Cartwright, you're incorrigible."

He leaned down and tenderly kissed my stomach.

"With you, always. You never said what happened with Elspeth's reading yesterday."

"Everything is fine with the babes. They're growing fast.

It should only be a few more weeks before we welcome our daughters into the world."

His head jerked up from where he'd set his ear on my belly.

"Daughters? Truly?"

I nodded, smiling at his excitement.

"I will spoil them as no father ever has," he vowed. "They will know my unconditional love. And will choose men for their merit rather than their wallet. Like their mother."

I laughed.

"Perhaps. Perhaps they will be like their father and have a fascination with gold coins."

He grinned at me.

Atwell was truly a trader's son. He was keen with his coin and seemed to have a sixth sense for how to double it. But I knew where his passion lay. I ran my fingers through his hair and let him love me with infinite care. No matter how large I grew, I continued to find joy in his touch.

As I was lacing my dress, someone knocked on our door. I heard the low murmur of Atwell's voice as he answered. A moment later, he slipped into the bedroom.

"You've been summoned to the castle," he said, moving to help me right myself. "It seems urgent. I'll see you at dinner." He kissed my temple and gave me a push toward the kitchen.

I was surprised to see the royal carriage waiting

outside. The guard helped me inside and shut the door. Before I had even settled on the plush seat, the vehicle lurched forward. The pace of the horses made for a rough ride, and I set a hand on my rounded belly.

Whatever prompted this grueling ride had to be truly urgent.

"We're almost there. Get ready for a sudden stop," the guard yelled from the other side of the door.

No sooner had the coach jolted to a standstill than the door opened. A multitude of crows cried out, creating a din from seemingly nowhere. The guard offered his hand.

"We must hurry."

I ran with him as best I could, up the stairs and through the castle to the queen's private chambers. Winded, I held my side while he knocked then immediately opened the door.

I entered the surprisingly crowded room and understood what was happening in a glance.

The queen sat in a birthing chair. Her face sweaty and pale. Several women stood around her. Further back from the proceedings, Elspeth observed everything. She waved me to her side.

"Something is wrong," Elspeth whispered. "The midwives aren't able to find anything wrong with the babe or the mother, but the delivery isn't progressing like it should."

The queen's amulet flared brightly then died again. Outside, the crows called out.

"The attacks started last night shortly after she went into labor."

"And the crows?" I asked.

"The same time. Messengers, I believe. So the caster knows if the spell succeeds or fails."

The queen panted a few heavy breaths then called for Elspeth. One of the midwives tried speaking, but the queen raised her hand and waved her away.

"I've had enough of your efforts. It is obviously not working and is time to try something new."

The midwives bowed and hurried from the room.

Elspeth approached the queen, and I followed in her wake. The queen looked exhausted.

"Greydon's birth was long and difficult. He took many hours to emerge. This feels different. Elspeth, you've seen the amulet. Is something happening to my child?"

Elspeth set her hands on the queen's belly.

"I don't believe so, Your Majesty," Elspeth said. "I believe the amulet is protecting the babe just as it did every time I tried to use casting to determine its gender."

I thought of all the times Elspeth checked my babes in front of the queen. How I'd learned I carried twin girls and heard their hearts beat. None of the same spells had worked on the queen. Each time, the amulet had flashed and the spell had failed.

"I feel something is wrong," the queen said.

Elspeth motioned me forward and pointed to a bowl of water and cloth. I wet the cloth and cooled the queen's face as Elspeth spoke to her.

"What is wrong is that somehow, the one casting spells on you knows about the babe and that this child is trying to make its way into the world. For whatever reason, this caster is trying to disrupt that." Elspeth took the queen's hand. "You've been in seclusion for three months. How could anyone know the exact time?"

The queen's eyes narrowed, and she looked at all the midwives.

"Get out! All of you."

The women scurried from the room, and the queen looked at Elspeth the moment the door slammed.

"Speak freely. Tell me what you know."

"I always do, Your Majesty." She pulled an amulet from the bodice of her dress. "This is for the babe. The moment it appears, this will touch the babe's skin. I believe the caster is testing if it has appeared yet. The moment it does, the babe will likely die without this." She set the amulet aside and placed her hands on the queen's stomach again.

"I also believe the caster is disrupting your contractions to delay the delivery and sap your strength."

The queen closed her eyes for a moment.

"I cannot deny that I'm already exhausted."

"Let's remove you from the chair and place you on the bed. You can rest between contractions."

I helped Elspeth move the queen. We no sooner had her settled than the door to her room burst open. The king came striding in, worry on his face.

"Why have you dismissed the midwives?" he asked gently.

"One of them has spoken of this babe. Spells are being cast now that I am laboring to bring this child into the world."

The king frowned and looked at Elspeth with a hint of anger.

"It's not Elspeth, my love. You know that. Do not let your distaste for magic blind you. Not all who use it are bad."

During the months of her pregnancy, the queen had confided that prior to betrothing her, the king had almost been ensnared by another. One who used her magic to try to entrance him. He'd never forgotten the feeling of being controlled and resented all who used magic.

The king sighed and moved closer to Sevil, love on his face. When he again focused on Elspeth, his expression was clear of any anger toward her.

"Your Majesty, given what has happened in Turre and the attacks now centered on the queen, I believe you have the power to stop this madness."

"How so?"

"A proclamation that the queen is delivering your second heir. And your vow to never wed again should the queen die."

The king looked at his wife.

"I will not lose you."

"You won't," she said, holding his hand tightly.

"I believe the caster's plan is to stall the labor to drain the queen of strength. I cannot use my magic to directly counter the casting. However, Margaret can."

"I can?" I said as all eyes shifted to me.

"You and the queen share a bond already. Both of you are pregnant and have an affection for one another. It's a natural magic that we can use with the help of a small cut on your right hand and a small cut on the queen's left. You will lie beside her and hold her hands. Her pain will be your pain. Her exhaustion will be yours."

I understood what this meant. Blood magic. While not inherently bad, it could be dangerous. I hesitated and set a hand on my belly.

"The babes?" I asked.

"It is your strength the queen will use. However, the babes will be touched by the magic. I cannot say how that will affect them."

I looked at the queen, wanting so badly to help but terrified for my unborn children.

"No," she said. "I will not risk another woman's children for my own."

"You misunderstand," Elspeth said. "We're all born with a certain amount of ability. I don't know how being touched by this type of magic will affect their abilities or their futures. I do not foresee this magic risking their lives. Only your own."

The queen shook her head, and I took her hand.

"We should try. It is my duty as your friend and subject to give you what strength I can so you may deliver this babe before anyone realizes what we're doing."

The queen looked at the king.

"Elspeth is right. The proclamation should help."

A contraction ripped through her just then. She cried out and grabbed her stomach. As she did, the crows cried out, and the amulet flared to life. The queen panted through the pain, but I could see she was no longer focused on the babe but the amulet.

The king stroked his wife's head, a look of fear on his face, until the amulet stopped glowing and the contraction was gone.

"Do what you must," he said to Elspeth. "I will make the announcement as you say."

The queen caught his hand before he could leave.

"Amnesty for my friends. Margaret is risking everything to help me. She and her children shall be protected by the crown after this. For the rest of their lives."

"It shall be done," he said, kissing her brow.

As soon as he left, I grabbed one of the bandages and

had the queen sit up. I wrapped it crisscross her chest until I felt I had enough to cover the light, hopping it would worry her less if she couldn't see it. Then I crawled up into the bed next to her and waited for Elspeth to cut our palms.

"Do not let go," Elspeth warned us. "You risk the other's life if you do."

The queen and I nodded. When the next contraction came, we labored together. At first, it wasn't bad. I could feel the strength I was lending the queen. Then my belly started to tighten with hers, and I could feel the queen drawing my strength in greater need. It only took a handful of those before I too was resting my eyes between contractions.

"You're both doing nicely," Elspeth crooned, wiping our faces with a cool cloth. "I could see the babe's head on that last push."

The door to the room opened again, and the king strode in. He went to the queen and smoothed back her hair.

"It is done. Heralds are yelling the proclamation in the streets, and the scholars are making arrangements for the Cartwright family."

"Thank you," she said just before another contraction stole both our breaths.

"Your Majesty, I could use your help. Here is the babe's amulet. It needs to touch the babe's skin the moment its head is clear. Do you understand?"

I barely paid any attention to what happened next as a

flood of warmth gushed between my legs. I frowned and lifted my head.

"Should there be so much blood?" the king asked softly, looking between the queen's legs.

I realized that the warmth I felt wasn't my own. Instead of answering, Elspeth looked at me then my hand holding the queen's.

"Everything you have, Margaret."

I nodded, held tightly, and closed my eyes to focus on sending all my strength into the queen. I could feel myself grow weaker. The labor of each breath. The weariness that tugged at my consciousness, begging me to release my hold on this world.

"One more push, Your Majesty."

My stomach clenched at the same time I felt another flood of warmth between my legs. This time the pain was enough that I cried out.

"Stay strong, Margaret. Your babes will wait. Keep your grip firm, and think of the queen."

I knew then that the pain and wetness I felt weren't an echo of the queen's but my own. I struggled to hold on. To stay conscious. In my weariness, I briefly wished for Atwell.

Another pain ripped through me, and the queen and I cried out together. Elspeth and the king said something but I couldn't focus. I felt myself pulled deeper and deeper into the darkness.

From somewhere in the shadows, Sevil's voice reached me.

"I cannot take more from you, my sweet Margaret. You have my love and gratitude always."

The strain left me as did the feel of the queen's hand.

"Sevil, no!"

The king's roar made my ears ring. I turned my head to look at the queen's pale face. Her eyes were partially open, unfocused and unblinking.

The queen was dead.

EPILOGUE

LOST IN THOUGHT, I WATCHED THE SUN RISE FROM MY place in the sitting room. Although I'd just woken, I was tired already.

In all the years since the queen's passing, I'd never recovered. I recalled that day and how Elspeth had taken me home after I'd delivered my twin daughters in the queen's bed. Her words still rang in my ears.

"I'm sorry, Margaret. When the queen released you while the bond still held, she kept what strength you'd lended her. It will never return."

Exhausted from childbirth, I hadn't fully understood what that meant. And Elspeth had left Drisdall shortly after, robbing me of the opportunity to learn more.

I understood why she'd left. The king, in his grief, had banished any magic users he found. Those who refused to leave Drisdall were sent into the Dark Forest, a death sentence with all the beasts loose within the shadows there.

"Are you ready for me to read to you, Mother?" Kellen asked.

I looked at my dark-haired daughter and smiled.

"I'm ready."

I listened to the soft, sweet tone of her voice and felt blessed. At fifteen, she was stunningly beautiful. In that way, she and her sister, Eloise were the same. In so many other ways, they differed.

One was fire and passion, her temper igniting like a cinder on dried grass. The other was quiet and distant, yet strong like a snow laden forest. Kellen was my snow and moon. Cool and distant, but no less loving of her parents. Eloise was my fire and sun. Her temper sparked often, but her light brought life to the room whenever she entered.

"Mother? Would you like to rest? You seem tired today."

I offered my hand to my daughter. Her strong, warm fingers wrapped around mine.

"Only lost in wonder at my two beautiful children. But perhaps I should rest."

Kellen kissed my cheek and left the room. I returned my attention to the sun-dappled trees outside the window. Gifted this land by the king, Atwell and I had raised our girls in peace and prosperity.

I was grateful for each day with my family. Yet, something told me those days were drawing to an end. It wasn't only my progressive weakness, which was keeping Atwell away longer and longer as he sought magical cures. Something deep within me said my time drew near. A knowing unlike anything I'd felt before. And that knowing told me my death wouldn't be natural.

A storm was coming. And it would rob me of what little life I still possessed. But it wasn't my life that really mattered. It never had. It was always about the two babes I was meant to bring into this world. The daughters who were touched by magic both light and dark.

While the knowing told me my story was almost at an end, it also said the story of my children was just beginning.

AND SO BEGINS the Tales of Cinder and the Tales of Snow...

THANK YOU FOR READING DISOWNED, *a prequel novella to the upcoming Tales of Cinder! I'm so excited to dive into another fairy tale world (If you haven't already checked out the Beastly Tales, you should!). If you want to learn more about the Tales of Cinder and Tales of Snow, be sure to sign up for my newsletter at https://mjhaag.melissahaag.com. Or, you can order Defiant, Tales of Cinder, book 1, now! Https://mjhaag.melissahaag.com/project/defiant Happy reading!*

AUTHOR'S NOTE

Thank you for reading Disowned! It was wonderful to jump back into the world I created for the Beastly Tales. While Beauty and the Beast is my favorite fairy tale, by far; Cinderella is easily my sister-in-law's favorite. Because I love her, and all the readers who wanted more, writing the Tales of Cinder was an easy decision. I hope my take on the well-retold tale will make everyone laugh, cry, and want to hurt a character or two. :)

Disowned is just a taste of what's to come. While Defiant might start out light, the trilogy will get dark quickly and it perfect for readers to love a dark fantasy. I can't wait to share it with everyone!

If you want to keep up to date on what I'm working on, sign up for my newsletter at mjhaag.melissahaag.com/subscribe or join my facebook fan group, MJ's Curvy Cartel. Hope to see you there!

Happy reading!

Melissa

CHARACTER LIST

Margaret Thoning - The girl who saves the kingdom.

Atwell Cartwright - Margaret's love interest.

Judith - A housemaid.

Elsepth - The caster and Margaret's mentor and friend.

Aftan - The King of Drisdall

Sevil - The Queen of Drisdall.

Greyden - Young prince of Drisdall.

Eloise - Twin daughter of Margaret and Atwell.

Kellen - Twin daughter of Margaret and Atwell.

This is a prequel to the Tales of Cinder, which takes part in the Beastly Tales world. If you haven't yet read the Beastly Tales, you're missing out on a seductively dark Beauty and the Beast retelling. There's character cross over between the two trilogies that you're going to love.

EXCERPT FROM DEFIANT

Now Available!

The sudden baying of hounds startled the chickens at my feet.

"Hugh?" I called, shaking the grain dust from my apron.

"Here, Miss Eloise." Our groomsman appeared from the stable, leading Sugar by her reins.

"Does that sound like hunting dogs?"

"It does." He nimbly leapt onto Sugar's back. "I'll go warn the hunters away."

As Hugh rode down the rutted path leading away from our small estate, I turned toward the two-storied house I called home. Smoke curled from all four chimneys, but with the hint of spring in the crisp air, I knew the fires wouldn't be necessary for long.

Letting myself into the kitchen, I inhaled the warm yeasty smell of the bread dough Judith was kneading.

"Were those hounds we heard?" she asked.

"Yes. Hugh went to warn the owners off." I shrugged out of my cloak and hung it and my apron by the door.

"It's been happening too frequently in recent years. The king should remind people that he cares about these lands by visiting them more often." Judith, who'd been with our family since I'd been born sixteen years ago, knew just how infrequently the king left his castle.

"I'm sure he has bigger concerns with Prince Granger's negotiations in the north," I said.

"What could we possibly need from the north?" Anne asked as she set a tray with a tea service for three.

"My guess is wool," Judith said. "In those colder temperatures, the herds probably have thicker coats."

While they spoke, I inspected the tray for something to eat.

"I was about to take this to the sitting room," Anne said, noting my interest. "Mrs. Cartwright requested you join her and your sister in there."

"You know Mother would be upset if she heard you calling her that," I said. "You're supposed to use her given name, Margaret."

"In her presence," Anne said with a small smile. "Elsewhere, I'll respectfully use her title."

I followed Anne from the kitchen, glad that Mother had selected her out of the many who had applied for the position. Already a widow, Anne was only two years older than me and didn't want anything other than security in life. Something Mother wanted for Kellen and myself. Something I had no interest in if it came in the form of a husband.

From the study, I heard the soft murmur of Kellen's voice as she read to Mother. She paused when Anne and I entered the room.

Mother reclined on a settee by the window. Although the sunlight gave her pale skin a healthier glow, the blankets that covered her body and pillows that propped her head bespoke the true state of her well-being. Yet, as much as Mother lived the life of an invalid, her gaze still alertly found mine.

"Hounds again?" she asked.

"So it seems," I answered, taking the seat near her.

Kellen shut her book and looked at me. My twin was my opposite in almost every way. Her straight ebony hair contrasted with my wavy golden tresses. The startling blue of her eyes, as well as her pale skin, held no warmth, whereas my golden tones were reflected in the warm hazel of my gaze. While I was quick to let the world know every emotion I felt, she held everything inside. I also towered over her petite frame by four inches, which I never used to my advantage. I never had to because Kellen and I didn't fight. Ever. Our differences did not make me love my sister less. No, I loved her more for each one.

I leaned forward and placed a kiss on my mother's soft cheek, surprising her.

"What's that for?"

"For giving me a sister instead of a brother. She would have been beastly as a boy."

"I would have been too small to be beastly," Kellen said evenly. "And tormented for my manly inadequacies. The only safe thing Mother could do for me was make me a girl."

Mother snorted, a smile ghosting her lips, our banter amusing her as I'd hoped it would.

"Speaking of manly attributes...did either of you notice any of interest when you went to market?" she asked. "I'd rather hoped there would be callers soon."

I gave Kellen a side glance. She kept her gaze focused on Mother.

"What?" Mother asked, catching the look. "What happened?"

"Nothing of importance, Mother," Kellen said. She looked at Anne, who'd been preparing our tea, and accepted the first cup for Mother. The milky brown liquid was laced with medicine.

"I won't drink that until you girls tell me what happened," Mother said. The surly note in her words made me smile.

"Well, we know it's not Father who gave me my temper," I said.

"You're right," Mother said, relaxing visibly. "It is better to nurture kindness in every thought and deed than to let even a cinder of anger smolder in your soul. For it only takes a cinder to start a fire." Then, she looked at me, love reflecting in her gaze.

"A fire can easily destroy what it took a lifetime to build."

"Or the face of a shopkeeper's son," Kellen added.

Mother made a pained expression.

"Oh, Eloise, what did you do?"

"I tested the sturdiness of the blacksmith's newest frying pan. I'm happy to report the smith was quite pleased with the results."

"You hit a boy with a frying pan?"

"Well, if you must put it so brashly...yes."

Anne made a small noise and quickly excused herself.

Mother stared at me for a moment before taking her tea from Kellen and drinking it down in several long swallows. She handed back the cup and closed her eyes.

"I'm ready for the full adventurous tale, my darlings."

Kellen and I shared a smile and launched into a recounting of our market visit from the day before. We embellished a few places for entertainment purposes, but never so much as to veer from the truth. The truth being that, years ago, Kellen and I had gradually gained a reputation of sorts with the boys in town. My quick to ignite temper had earned me the nickname of Cinder while Kellen's abidingly cool exterior had earned her the name Snow.

"When Carver lobbed a ball of muddy snow at Kellen, I grabbed the pan to block it; but my aim was off. While the ball splattered us, the pan hit Carver with a resounding gong that gained the attention of just about everyone on the street."

Mother snorted a laugh and held out both of her hands without opening her eyes. The tea always made her tired.

Kellen took one, and I took the other. Mother's thin fingers felt so frail in my own.

"I have been blessed with two beautiful, headstrong daughters who not only know how to care for themselves but for others, too. Your beauty is not in the texture of your skin or the shine of your hair. It's what's inside each of you, and it's how you influence the world around us. You are my sun, Eloise. And you, my moon, Kellen. Both lights shine brightly and fill my life with joy."

She gave our hands a gentle squeeze.

"You would fill my life with more joy if one of those thick-headed miscreants had caught your fancy, though."

She peeked at us from under the lashes of one eye before closing it again.

"I hardly believe a miscreant—"

"Or a band of them," Kellen added.

"—is what you had in mind for our future spouses," I said.

Mother sighed.

"Too right you are. A handsome man with a good heart and steadfast loyalty, like your father, is what I hope for both of you. Go now. I need to rest. Anne dosed my tea again. Tell her this concoction tasted like shite from the yard."

I choked on my laugh while Kellen shook her head.

While Mother rested, we took the tray to the kitchen.

"How is she today?" Judith asked.

"The same," Kellen said. "Dying."

"Aren't we all?" Judith said, not put out by Kellen's bluntness. "Some of us just take longer going about it and don't see it for what it is. The end comes for all of us, Kellen. It's what we do with the days we have that matters."

Kellen nodded and grabbed her cloak. I did the same. Side by side, we walked down the hill toward town. Just before the path met the larger road, we took a small walking trail to the right and started the trek up the rocky incline. Neither of us spoke until we reached the top. There, we stood near the edge and looked out over Towdown.

"Mother received a letter from Father yesterday. He's due to return soon," Kellen said.

Mother hated when Father had to leave. However, given his profession, he left often.

"I don't blame him," Kellen said when I didn't speak.

I turned to look at my sister.

"For staying away," she clarified even though I knew my sister well enough to guess most of her thoughts.

The world might see Kellen's steady, light blue gaze and bland expression as being unfeeling. But, I knew better. I saw her expression for what it was. A mask to hide the pain. It hurt her to see Mother like this...almost as much as it hurt Father.

Wrapping my arms around Kellen, I stared down at the rooftops and the lazy spirals of smoke hazing the air. The din from town didn't reach us, and the wind kept all but the barest hint of smoke from the air. Just beyond the rooftops, I could see the glimmer of white stone in the sun. The castle.

With a sigh, Kellen placed her head on my shoulder and wrapped her arms around my waist in return.

"Mother knows we all love her deeply. That's why she hired Anne," I said. "She hopes we will leave when the time is right."

"Since marriage appeals to you as little as it appeals to me, I doubt either of us is going anywhere," Kellen said. "Having Anne here hasn't changed that."

"Mother's hope will continue, regardless."

Kellen lifted her head and stepped away from me.

"What does the future hold for us?" she asked.

"Spinsterhood, most likely. Nothing too terrifying," I said.

The faint pounding of hooves drew our attention.

"We'd better get back," she said.

I followed her down the familiar trail. By the time we made it to the stable, Hugh had already unsaddled Sugar.

"Was there any trouble?" I asked.

"None. The hounds don't belong to hunters. They belong to the Crown. It seems the Royal Retreat is due for a visit."

Kellen and I shared a look. I could barely recall the last time the rambling estate, a bit further up the hill, had been used. It had been at least five years ago. Neither Kellen nor I had gotten a glimpse of the royal entourage during the king's week-long visit then. We'd been strictly forbidden from leaving our small estate.

"We must tell Mother," Kellen said.

Judith was absent from the kitchen, but a small roast spit over the fire said she would return soon. I inhaled deeply.

"Stop smelling dinner, Eloise, and tie your shoes," Kellen said without rancor.

"This is why you're four inches shorter. If you don't appreciate your food, you don't grow."

She snorted, and I knew I'd amused her even if her face didn't show it.

Together, we went to the parlor. Anne was sitting quietly in the corner, reading from a primer.

"How are your studies?" Kellen asked.

"Well and good," Anne said. "I would like to try reading

to her tomorrow."

Kellen nodded. It was Kellen's job to read to mother in the morning. I read in the afternoon. Or sang. Or played the piano. Whatever mother seemed to want. She'd scolded us often that we need not wait on her or entertain her. Kellen was always quick to say that we weren't entraining her but honing our entertainment skills for our future endeavors. Since Mother always had marriage on her mind, the answer usually appeased her.

Anne put her primer away and left us to sit and wait for Mother to wake. Her afternoon naps usually only lasted an hour or two.

When she opened her eyes, she smiled at us.

"Did you watch me sleep long?" she asked.

"Ages," I answered. "One doesn't often see a sleeping princess."

Her smile widened.

"Speaking of royalty," Kellen said. "It seems the hounds belong to the king. He has finally decided to visit his royal retreat."

The royal retreat was more than just a massive stretch of land north of Towdown. It was also the name of the sprawling home the royal family used for some time away from the castle.

"This is not good news," Mother said, looking concerned. "It would be best if you stayed out of the woods while the king is in residence at the retreat."

Most mama's would be excited, especially since we lived on royal land and were allowed to hunt it when others were not. Not our Mother.

"I cannot imagine needing two homes," I said, trying to distract her from the worry in her eyes. "It's not fun cleaning one."

"Do honestly think his highness cleans anything?" Kellen asked, an aloof note in her voice.

I grinned.

"Certainly his privy. It wouldn't be fair to ask someone else to do that."

Kellen nudged me with her elbow and I realized what I'd said. Mother used nothing but a chamber pot that Anne, Kellen, or I cleaned every day.

"They would rob him blind," I added smoothly.

"How so?" Kellen asked.

"Come now. It's obvious." I paused for a moment and glanced between Mother and Kellen. "His shite is gold."

Mother burst out laughing and Kellen shook her head.

"Eloise, I hope that you find your beau soon."

"Why is that, Mother?"

"Because you'll soon out swear him. A lady shouldn't speak so."

"Too right. But any man worthy of my interest will need to take me as I am. Filthy mouth and all."

"There is a delivery boy," she said.

"Send him in," Mother said.

Anne disappeared, and a few moments later, a youth walked in. He was dressed in neat trousers and a coat that was just a tad too short for his wrists. A common sight for growing boys. His gaze swept over the three of us, and he removed the floppy red cap with a gold emblem on it from his shaggy dark head to give a precise, small bow.

"Can we help you?" Mother asked.

"Yes, ma'am. I have a delivery for Mrs. Cartwright." He lifted the small, brown paper-wrapped package he held.

"I am she," Mother said.

The boy came forward.

"A coin, Kellen," Mother said.

Kellen gave the boy a copper in exchange for the package. With a bob of his head, he returned to Anne, who I knew would see him out.

Mother smiled in excitement as Kellen handed her the package. The gifts that Father always sent made his absence less cruel. Each one let us know he was thinking of us.

"I should wait until he returns to open it," she said.

I grinned.

"At least, until yours arrive," she added. Her eyes never left the package.

"He sent yours ahead of his arrival for a reason," Kellen said. "Open it. We want to see what it is."

Mother didn't need any further encouragement. She tugged the string free and removed the paper to expose a small, cloth-covered box. We all gasped when she removed the lid to reveal a gold encased emerald pendant strung on a delicate gold chain.

"Your father's latest venture must have done very well," Mother said, breathlessly.

She lifted the chain and let the pendant dangle in the sunlight. It almost seemed to glow with a light of its own.

"It's beautiful," Kellen said.

"Help me put it on. I want your father to see me wearing it when he returns."

Kellen stood and helped Mother ease the chain over her hair then rearranged her braid prettily to lay over one shoulder.

"There," she said, moving back.

The sunlight, streaming in through the window, reflected against the stone; and an unnatural green light flashed in Mother's eyes briefly as she looked at me.

"What do you think?" she asked.

"You've never been more beautiful," Kellen said when I hesitated.

She smiled and blinked heavily.

"I believe this gift overexcited me. I need to rest for a bit."

She didn't rest, though. She exhaled loudly, her lids half closing.

"Mother?" I said, standing to touch her face. "Mother?"

She didn't respond.

"I don't think she's breathing, Eloise," Kellen said softly.

THE BEASTLY TALES

Beauty and the Beast with seductively dark twists!

BOOK 1: DEPRAVITY

When impoverished, beautiful Benella is locked inside the dark and magical estate of the beast, she must bargain for her freedom if she wants to see her family again.

BOOK 2: DECEIT

Safely hidden within the estate's enchanted walls, Benella no longer has time to fear her tormentors. She's too preoccupied trying to determine what makes the beast so beastly. In order to gain her freedom, she must find a way to break the curse, but first, she must help him become a better man while protecting her heart.

BOOK 3: DEVASTATION

Abused and rejected, Benella strives to regain a purpose for her life, and finds herself returning to the last place she ever wanted to see. She must learn when it is right to forgive and when it is time to move on.

Becareful what you wish for...

PREQUEL: DISOWNED

In a world where the measure of a person rarely goes beneath the surface, Margaret Thoning refuses to play by its rules. She walks away from everything she's ever known to risk her heart and her life for the people who matter most.

BOOK 1: DEFIANT

When the sudden death of Eloise's mother points to forbidden magic, Eloise's life quickly goes from fairy tale to nightmare. Kaven, the prince's manservant, is Eloise's prime suspect. However, when dark magic is used, nothing is as simple as it seems.

BOOK 2: DISDAIN

Cursed to silence, Eloise is locked in the tattered remains of her once charming life. The smoldering spark of her anger burns for answers and revenge. However, games of magic can have dire consequences.

BOOK 3: DAMNATION

With the reason behind her mother's death revealed, Eloise must prevent her stepsisters from marrying the prince and exact her revenge. However, a secret of the royal court strikes a blow to her plans. Betrayed, Eloise will question how far she's willing to go for revenge.

THE
RESURRECTION
CHRONICLES

Humor, romance, and sexy dark fey!

BOOK 1: DEMON EMBER

In a world going to hell, Mya must learn to accept help from her new-found demon protector in order to find her family as a zombie-like plague spreads.

BOOK 2: DEMON FLAMES

As hellhounds continue to roam and the zombie plague spreads, Drav leads Mya to the source of her troubles—Ernisi, an underground Atlantis and Drav's home. There Mya learns that the shadowy demons, who've helped devastate her world, are not what they seem.

BOOK 3: DEMON ASH

While in Ernisi, cites were been bombed and burned in an attempt to stop the plague. Now, Marauders, hellhounds, and the infected are doing their best to destroy what's left of the world. It's up to Mya and Drav to save it.

BOOK 4: DEMON ESCAPE

While running from zombies, hellhounds, and the people who kept her prisoner, Eden encounters a new creature. He claims he only wants to protect her. Eden must decide who the real devils are between man and demon, and choosing wrong could cost her life.

BOOK 5: DEMON DECEPTION

Grieving from the loss of her husband and youngest child, Cassie lives in fear of losing her remaining daughter. To gain protection, Cassie knows she needs to sleep with one of the dark fey and give him the one thing she isn't sure she can. Her heart.

THE
RESURRECTION
CHRONICLES

The apocalyptic adventure continues!

BOOK 6: DEMON NIGHT

Angel's growing weaker by the day and needs help. In exchange for food, she agrees to give Shax advice regarding how to win over Hannah. If Angel can help make that happen, just maybe she won't be kicked out when her fellow survivors find out she's pregnant.

BOOK 7: DEMON DAWN

In a post-apocalyptic world, Benna is faced with the choice of trading her body and heart to the dark fey in order to survive the infected.

BOOK 8: DEMON DISGRACE

Hannah is drinking away her life to stanch the bleeding pain from past trauma. Merdon, a dark fey with a violent history, relentlessly sets out to show her there's something worth living for.

BOOK 9: DEMON FALL

June never planned to fall in love. She had her eyes on the prize: a career and independence. Too bad the world ended and stole those options from her. Maybe falling in love had been the better choice after all.

www.ingramcontent.com/pod-product-compliance
Lightning Source LLC
Chambersburg PA
CBHW021958190626
46808CB00017B/2511